Serhiy Zhadan

# DEPECHE MODE

Glagoslav Publications

Depeche Mode

By Serhiy Zhadan

First published in Ukrainian as
"Депеш мод" in 2004 by Folio

Translated from the Ukrainian by Myroslav Shkandrij



Glagoslav Publications Ltd
88-90 Hatton Garden
EC1N 8PN London
United Kingdom

www.glagoslav.com

ISBN: 978-1-909156-84-5

# Contents

*The referee's completely pissed*
*he doesn't like our Metalist*

*15.02.04 (Sunday)*

When I was fourteen and had my own views about life, I first loaded up on alcohol. Up to the gills. It was really hot and the blue heavens swam above me, and I lay dying on a striped mattress and couldn't even get drunk, because I was only fourteen and simply didn't know how. In the last fifteen years, I've had more than enough reasons to dislike this life: from the beginning, from when I first began to become aware of it, it seemed a vile and mean thing, it immediately began creating lousy situations that you try not to remember but cannot forget. For my part, of course, I never made any special demands, my relations with life were okay, in spite of its clinically idiotic nature. For the most part, unless there was some new governmental initiative, I was satisfied—with the circumstances in which I lived, the people I knew, the ones I saw from time to time and had dealings with. For the most part they didn't bother me, and, I expect, didn't bother them. What else? I was satisfied with how much money I had, which is not to say that I was satisfied with the amount as such —I never really had any dough at all—but I was satisfied with the basic principle of how it circulated around me—from childhood I noticed that banknotes appear when you need them, roughly in the bare minimum required, and normally things worked out: they work out fine, of course, if you haven't lost all sense of decency and at least keep up some appearances—meaning that you brush your teeth, or don't eat pork if you're a Muslim; then the angel with black accountant armbands and dandruff on his wings appears with strange regularity to refill your current account with a certain sum in local currency, just enough, on the one hand, to prevent you from croaking and, on the other, to stop you from screwing around too much and messing up your reincarnation by buying tankers of oil or cisterns of spirits. I was satisfied with this arrangement, I understood the angels and supported them. I was satisfied with the country in which I lived, the amount of shit that filled it, which in the most critical aspects of my life in this country reached up to my knees and higher. I understood that I could very well have been born in another far worse country, with, for example, a harsher climate or an authoritarian form of government ruled not simply by bastards, like in my country, but by demented bastards who pass on their rule to their children along with a foreign debt and domestic obscurantism. So I considered my fate not to be so bad, and I didn't worry too much about these things. For the most part I was satisfied with everything, I was satisfied with the television picture I saw through the windows of the apartments in which I lived, which is why I tried not to change the channel too quickly, because I had noticed that attention from the reality installed around me always resulted in some predictable nastiness or simply more of life's routine crap. Reality on its own is cool, but it's a complete bummer once you start going over the post-game statistics, when you analyze your own and reality's major indicators and see that it committed more fouls than you did but only your side got penalized. If anything really oppressed me it was the television screen's constant, insistent demands for unnatural sexual relations with me—to put it simply, to screw me by taking advantage of my social rights and Christian duties. I've lived my fifteen years of adult life cheerfully, taking no part in the construction of civil society, never turning up at a polling site, and successfully avoiding contact with the oppressive regime, if you know what I mean. I had no interest in politics, no interest in economics, no interest in culture, no interest even in the weather forecast—this was maybe the only thing in the country that inspired trust, but I had no interest in it anyway.

Now I'm thirty. What has changed in the last fifteen years? Almost nothing. Even the external appearance of this… president hasn't changed much; in any case his portraits are airbrushed today in the same way as they were before, even I noticed that. The music on the radio has changed, but by and large I don't listen to the radio. Clothes have changed, but the eighties, as far as I can tell, are still in fashion. Television hasn't changed, it's still as sticky and irritating as lemonade spilled on a parquet floor. The climate hasn't changed, the winters are just as long, and the springs just as long-awaited. Friends have changed, meaning that some have disappeared forever, and others have appeared to take their place. Memory has changed—it has become longer, but not any better. I hope there will be enough of it for about another sixty years of extended pragmatic apathy and unshakeable equanimity of spirit, which is what I wish for myself. Amen.

*17.06.93 (Thursday)*

## INTRODUCTION NO. 1

*16.50*

June 17, near five in the afternoon, Dogg Pavlov tries to enter the subway. He walks up to the revolving door, goes straight up to the woman in uniform, and pulls a veteran's card out of his pocket. The woman in uniform looks at the card and reads "Pavlova, Vira Naumivna." "So?" she asks.

"My grandmother," says Dogg Pavlov.

"Where is your grandmother?"

"This," says Dogg pointing at the card, "is my grandmother."

"What of it?"

"She's a veteran."

"And you, what do you want?"

"She burned in a tank."

The woman looks at the card again. Who knows, she thinks, maybe she did burn—you can't tell from a photograph.

"Well, okay," she says. "And what can I do for you?'"

"A pass," says Dogg.

"You burned in a tank too?"

"Listen," Dogg begins to bargain. "Maybe I'm bringing her something to eat."

"What do you mean, to eat?"

"You know, to eat." Dogg tries to remember what his grandmother eats when she is given food. "Dairy products—cheese, for example."

"You're a cheese yourself," says the lady in uniform without animosity.

Dogg understands how all this looks from the side: he's beating his head against an enormous endless wall that separates him from life, beating his head without any hope of success, and all life's pleasures, including a ride on the subway, are just not in the cards right now, that's the way it looks. He gathers all his willpower into his fist and says something like: Listen, lady—of course, he doesn't say it in those words, but the content is approximately the same. So listen to me carefully—he says—okay? Listen, listen, I want to say something else, listen. Well, in spite of—let's see, how can I say it—you, I don't know, you can take this in your own way, I agree, maybe it means nothing to you but still you have to agree: my grandmother cannot be allowed to die of hunger just because I, her beloved grandson, if you allow me, was denied entry to the subway by some lousy rear guarder. You have to agree, no? (Well, at this point they just lay into one another verbally, but we'll ignore that.) He concentrates all his willpower and suddenly dives under the woman's arms, waving the veteran's card in the air, and disappears into the subway's cool intestines.

"What does he mean, lousy rear guarder who never saw the front lines?" thinks the woman. "I wasn't born 'til 1949."

*17.10*

At the stadium stop, Dogg gets off onto an empty platform; in about an hour Metalist is playing its last home game, everyone is getting together, you know how it is, the end of the season, the rainy summer above, the clouded sky and the dilapidated stadium that stands somewhere just above Dogg; in the last few years it's started to come apart, grass springing up between the concrete slabs, especially after a rain, the stands covered in pigeon shit, there's shit on the field too, especially when our team's playing, the country's in ruins, the phys ed movement is in ruins, the big chiefs have fucking wasted the main thing—in my opinion, whatever you say—because under the Sovs there were two things that you could be proud of, the soccer championship and nuclear weapons, and the guys who took these pleasures away from the people will hardly live to a peaceful and carefree old age, for surely nothing undermines karma as much as screwed-up national politics. Dogg stands on the platform a bit longer, his friends are supposed to come from the other direction, so he just has to wait for them. Dogg is tired and worn out, he's been drinking for three days, and the weather's bad too, obviously the weather is affecting him, the pressure or whatever it's called—what do you call the condition when you drink for three days and suddenly stop recognizing your friends and family? It's the pressure, obviously.

He can't even remember what happened—the summer had begun so well, the rains came, Dogg was successfully pissing away the best years of his life, when suddenly his advertising friends dragged the reliably unemployed Dogg into the bowels of the advertising industry: to put it more simply, they hired him as a courier in their newspaper's advertising department. Dogg suffered badly, but he held up and kept going to work. He wasn't much benefit to them, but at least someplace considered him human, although personally he has never been very concerned about this—well, what are friends for, if not to straighten out your social status through direct intervention. I said from the first that he wouldn't last long but they weren't listening, they said don't worry, on the whole he's a decent guy, a bit fucked up, but okay, okay, and I agreed, okay.

Dogg lasts ten days, after that he goes on a binge and doesn't come to work anymore, and so as not to be found he drinks at the homes of acquaintances; at 19 he knows half the city, one night he even sleeps at the railway station—there he meets some mushroom-picking friends who are taking the early-morning commuter train to somewhere in the Donbas for raw material and spends the night with them under the columns on the street, where he is rousted three times by the patrols; he sticks it out until morning, listening to tales about mushrooms and other thermonuclear stuff, then he breaks down and takes off for home. Here he encounters a ringing telephone. Under different circumstances Dogg would never have picked it up, but cold silver trout are already swimming inside him after a three-day alcoholic binge and their tails are beating against his kidneys and liver so painfully that his world is getting hazy and so he automatically picks up the receiver. "Dogg?" they shout into the telephone. "Don't you dare put down the phone!" His friends the advertisers Vova and Volodia, who fixed him up with the job in the advertising business to their own detriment, are sitting somewhere in their Komsomol office tearing the receiver from each other's hands trying to convince Dogg to speak to them, occasionally drifting off into profanities. "Dogg!" they say, "the main thing—don't you dare put down the phone. Hey asshole!" they say, reassured that he is listening. "If you put down the phone now, you're dead. We'll bury you, you hear?" "Hello," says Dogg in reply. "What do you mean 'hello'?" say Vova and Volodia losing their cool. "What do you mean 'hello'? Can you hear us?" "Yes," says the frightened Dogg. "Good," Vova and Volodia answer, encouraged. "Okay, listen, it's now ten in the morning." "What?" Dogg is now finally terrified and lets the receiver drop. The telephone immediately crackles again. He picks up the receiver indecisively. "You!!!" roars the voice. "Asshole!!! Don't you dare put down the phone!!!" Dogg swallows with difficulty. "Do you hear?" "Okay," says Dogg uncertainly. "So it's like this," explode the advertisers. "It is now ten in the morning—don't you dare put down the phone!!! You hear??? Don't you dare put down the phone!!! It's now ten. At half past five we'll be waiting for you by the stadium. If you don't come, we'll rip your balls off. If you come, we'll rip your balls off anyway. But it will be better for you if you come. Understand?" "Yes," says Dogg. "Do you understand!?" the advertisers cannot calm down. "I understand," says Dogg Pavlov, feeling the trout swimming cheerfully somewhere under his throat. "What's with you?" the advertisers finally ask. "Are you feeling bad?" "Yes." "Do you need anything?" "Some vodka." "Asshole," say Vova and Volodia and put down the receiver. Dogg takes a breath. Ten o'clock. He needs to change or have a drink, better a drink, of course. His granny comes out of the next room. This granny, he loves her and all that, even goes around with her veteran's card, you could even say that he's proud of her, not entirely, of course, but up to a certain point, he tells people that she burned in a tank, I have trouble imagining the little old lady in a tank wearing a helmet, although anything's possible. "How are you Vitalik?" she says. "Work, granny, work," says Dogg. "What kind of work is it?" worries the little old lady. "Yesterday, they telephoned all day, asking, 'Where is that asshole?' And I should know?"

*17.22*

Vova and Volodia jump out of the subway and meet up with Dogg, and they emerge onto the street. You alive? they ask. Dogg is completely pale, can't get it together; they drag him into the grocery store on Plekhanov Street and buy two bottles of vodka, don't worry, they tell Dogg, first we're going to bring you back to life and then we'll rip your balls off, there's no fun in ripping something off in your state, look at yourself; they take him up to the store window, the grocery is dark and empty, like most of the country's stores during this difficult time—they've brought the country to ruin, the bastards—look, they say to Dogg, look at yourself. Dogg is quite weak, he looks through the window and sees a waitress in a white coat who is also looking through the glass at a couple of jerks who look like dropouts standing on the street directly in front of her. They're holding up a third guy just like them and are pointing at her. She looks at them with contempt; Dogg somehow focuses his eyes, recognizes his reflection and suddenly notices inside this reflection a strange creature in white clothing who is wearing a large amount of makeup on her face and moving with difficulty within the confines of his body, as though trying to break out from inside him, and he begins to feel nauseous. Of course, thinks Dogg, that's my soul, but how come it's got gold teeth?

*17.35–18.15*

They spend forty minutes reviving Dogg. They pour vodka into him and in accordance with some law of physics as Dogg fills up with it he floats to the surface, greets everybody, all present also greet him—welcome back pioneer and hero Dogg Pavlov, great to have you back with us, we missed you, and Oh, says everyone, meaning Vova and Volodia, we simply needed to revive you so we could look once more into your honest if drunken eyes, so that you could tell us why you hate the advertising business in general and us, Volodia and me—says Vova—in particular; what did we do to make you take off without a word, with, by the way, a very important piece of correspondence, on account of which we would, if we could, rip your balls off twice. In this way a kind of friendly conversation takes place between them, you know how it is, and Dogg fully returns to the world, after his own soul had almost pushed him out of it, look around and listens: the trout are lying somewhere on the bottom, the angry gold-toothed angel in the white coat and nylon stockings has also flown off, the advertisers Vova and Volodia have dragged him somewhere into the bushes behind some white metal kiosks and are giving him generous helpings of vodka. Compromises are required in the social mode of existence.

*18.15*

Why do they never make it to the stadium on time for the pre-game inspirational music and opening speeches by municipal clerks? First of all, as a rule they arrive less than completely sober and therefore lack a clear idea of the time; sometimes they lack any clear idea whatsoever, not just about the time of day but even the season of the year, they're invariably in warm sweaters under the hot sun or in wet T-shirts during the first snow. Second, there's always some kind of lottery draw before the game and they categorically do not believe in lotteries. Third, as, you can understand, when you're 19 and you crawl into your section of the stadium and everyone—including the police—can see your wonderful, elated condition, what can be more uplifting? Later, when you grow up and start working in a bank or the offices of the gas utility, when you interact with reality through television, and with your friends by fax—if you have any friends, that is, and provided they, too, have a fax machine—then, naturally, you won't give a good God-damn about crazy drunk teenage hijinks that empty out your wallet and throw you into every plate-glass window in the world, a time when excitement moistens your eyes and the blood stops flowing under your fingernails because several hundred people are watching them entering their section, searching for their places, and carrying someone on their shoulders, calling him a dog for some reason, losing him from time to time among the benches, but then stubbornly and energetically picking him up and dragging him to their assigned places, away from the guards, away from the women selling ice cream, and in general away from the soccer, as they themselves conceive it.

*18.25*

Dogg Pavlov revives one more time at the stadium, it's good to sit like this with your friends, he thinks, on a bench somewhere under trees that rustle and sway in every direction, no, he suddenly thinks, they're not trees, what are they then?

A few sections over to the left, the opposing team's fans stand under the heavy June rain. There are a few dozen of them, they arrived at the railway station in the morning and several patrols have been trailing after them all day. At the stadium they've been assigned their own section, where they forlornly wave their soaked flags. Just before half-time the locals, disappointed with the score and the weather, break through the fence and begin to beat them. From down below on the field, a company of trainee firefighters runs up. The police don't think of anything better to do than push everybody out of the stadium and so they begin to press the people toward the exit while the first half is still going on; obviously, everyone forgets about the game and begins to cheer for our guys in the stands, the players also take more interest in the fighting than in their own game, it's interesting, after all, and unpredictable, here on the field everything has been clear from the start—in the final minutes someone is bound to screw up and lose the game—but over in the stands, see, there's a real contest going on, a rugby game, now even the firefighters are taking a few hits, but then the first half ends and the players reluctantly make their way to the tunnel, the police drag off the last of the visitors, so when the game resumes their section is empty. Only trampled and torn banners lie heavily in puddles like fascist standards on Red Square, our survivors return delightedly to their sections, the most passionate and principled among them go off to the railway station to hunt for the visitors as they return home; and then, around the fifteenth minute of the second half, one visitor runs into the stands—some very young kid, disheveled and wet, where he was all this time is a mystery, he has definitely missed all the most interesting stuff—he runs in and sees the signs of a battlefield, the torn flags of his team and none of his friends; where are our guys?

he cries, turning to the suddenly silent stands, hey, where are all our guys?!—and no one can answer him. Everyone feels sorry for the kid, even the ultras are silent, having interrupted their endless "the referee's a prick," and look dejectedly at the visitor, feeling embarrassed in front of the kid—it wasn't really very sporting, was it?—and the kid looks up at the now quiet sections, at the wet field on which the teams are churning up the mud, and he looks at the cold and almost motionless sky, and he cannot understand what has happened, where are the boys, what have these clowns done with them, and he picks up the bent plastic trumpet that one of his fallen friends had been blowing, and suddenly begins blowing into it, making a shrill, tearful and desperate sound that astonishes everyone: he blows with his back turned to the field, to the ultras, and to the now silent and shamed firefighters, he blows a note familiar to him alone, loud and false, breathing into it all his courage, all his despair, all his purely boyish love of life.

*19.30*

In the rafters above the last rows the sleepy pigeons have grown accustomed to our team's defeats, they coo sleepily and live quietly, bothering no one, delightful wet flocks, but Dogg hears them through his dream, they appear to him in his alcoholic debility and pull him out of it; you know that strange condition in which you see the light ahead with one eye, and with the other—how do you explain this—with the other you see what can perhaps be called the other side of the light, well, you know, in a word when you are shown a lot all at once but are not in any condition to see anything. And you don't want to. That's why Dogg sinks to the cement floor and begins to crawl away toward the exit, crushing the husks of sunflower seeds, cigarette butts, and lottery tickets with his tired chest. He crawls up to the exit, gets to his feet, and shakily keeps going up and up, to the last row; he grasps onto the metal support and hangs off it in complete exhaustion—don't fall off into the stands and on top of the fans, if you do you'll need to say you're sorry, to talk to somebody, to say something, and then everyone will immediately sense how bad your breath smells and will immediately guess that you've been drinking, so the main thing is not to speak to anyone and not to turn to anyone and if you fall then definitely someone will talk to you then you won't get out of it they'll say that your breath smells bad they will definitely smell it at soon as they begin talking to you even if you turn away and talk to the side they'll smell it anyway unless you turn completely aside and speak that way—what should I say? what should I say so they don't notice? what should I tell them? Quickly, before they notice and say something—what will they say? they'll say why don't you say something? why aren't you shouting? Why am I not shouting? I need to shout, otherwise they'll notice that my breath smells badly they will say that my breath smells because I'm not shouting or they'll think that I'm drunk because I'm not shouting what should I be shouting? what should I be shouting? well, what, what should I be shouting? I have to ask someone I have to turn aside and ask or turn aside and shout then no one will notice anything in any case they won't notice with all this noise alright I'll shout something to the side no one will notice how my breath stinks but everyone will notice that I'm shouting that means I'm not drunk everything's okay this is an okay plan only what should I shout well what should I shout what are they all shouting? about the ref about the ref only to the side so they don't hear and so they still notice yes I have to shout and definitely about the ref then everything will be okay—and here our forward breaks away one-on-one with the goalkeeper and shoots, he just fucking blasts it as hard as he can, several thousand wet supporters go still, hold their collective breath, you might say, and at this moment behind their backs in the damp silence a desperate cry echoes:

"Ye-e-e-e-e-e-e-e-e-e-e-e-e-e-e-s!!! You-u-u-u-u-u-u-u-u-u-u-u-u-u-u-u-u-u-u!!!"

And the soaked fans in the nearest sectors turn their heads as though enchanted and see good-old Dogg Pavlov there, whom even all the dogs here know, which is to say every sergeant, he's hanging from the steel support completely exhausted, having turned let's call it his back to the stands, and is emitting a prolonged wail from somewhere into nowhere, or whatever you want to call it.

*19.45*

Why? Because you're not just some moron who has reconciled himself to the existing unjust state of things and the surrounding accumulated crap, because you're not prepared to tear at someone's throat all your life over the grub they've chewed up. Because, all things considered, you've got something to say if someone asks you about the things that are most important, so that's enough, thinks Dogg, or more exactly, he's actually in no condition to think anything like this, but if he could think at this moment, he, I suppose, would think this, and so he begins to climb up the beam that supports the roof, tearing off the old green paint and the dried birdshit with his fingernails, pushing himself up against the cold pipe, carefully pulling himself higher, transposing his feet on the ironwork, he climbs directly over the heads of the sergeants who have forgotten about him for the moment, over the heads of all his wet and drunken acquaintances, as many as are here, over the heads of Vova and Volodia. He even recognizes them and stops just above them, examining them from above, thinking, wow, fantastic, if I reach down with my hand I can pull both of them up here, and he reaches out and says something to them, without even noticing how bad his breath smells.

And here our team puts he the ball in the back of the net, and the wet throats roar: Sco-o-o-o-o-o-o-o-o-r-r-r-re!!!!!! Sco-o-o-o-o-o-o-o-o-r-r-r-re!!!!!!—they roar and from this roar hundreds and thousands of sleepy pigeons tear themselves out from their dreams and fly out like bullets from their perches nestled with feathers, earth, and lottery tickets, they fly out in a wave into the wet sky, and this wave breaks against Dogg Pavlov, and he can't hold on and goes flying down, dropping a few metres and flopping with a smack onto the bench right next to Vova and Volodia, who finally remember their comrade, turn and see him next to them, just where he should be.

"Oh, Dogg," shouts Vova.

"Dogg, we scored," shouts Volodia.

"Great," says Dogg and smiles for what is the first time in the last three days.

*19.50–08.00*

Vova and Volodia are afraid to show their IDs and therefore are not allowed to approach Dogg, who is being hospitalized; they explain that they're friends, even relatives, distant but relatives all the same, but are told that they should be ashamed to admit that Dogg is a relative and he is placed—drunk and sleepy—on a stretcher and then quickly pushed into the ambulance, for some reason they all think Dogg is injured and not drunk, this saves him, he's not killed on the spot, as required by the instruction manual of sergeants, officers, and cadets when they are called upon heroically to defend sports complexes, places of mass relaxation for the laboring class during soccer games, political meetings, and other satanic rituals of the sporting-instructional type. Some sergeant with a bleeding heart even comes up to the driver of the ambulance, writes down his name and station number, leaves him his own office telephone number and orders him to immediately rush the badly injured Dogg to hospital, and tomorrow, if there's nothing serious, to bring his patched-up body to them in the district police station for further laboratory tests, there they will establish what kind of Gagarin this is who has fallen out of the fucking sky onto their heads. The driver all but salutes, well, you know what I mean, and the ambulance disappears behind the stadium's green gates, its sirens scattering wet supporters in whose cheerful whirlpool Vova and Volodia disappear—victories require congregations and a joyful collective mass, toasts, and harmonious choral singing. It's only defeats, bitter personal defeats, that require nothing more than drunken medics and respiratory equipment that doesn't work, or, more accurately, works but no one knows how.

By morning Dogg has barfed all over the bedsheets he was wrapped up in and elicits a reaction of strong disgust from the medical staff. The nurses on duty attempt to telephone somewhere, to find those distant relatives who wanted to take this trash back at the stadium, but no one knows the telephone number, the only document they find on Dogg is a veteran's ID card in the name of Vira Naumivna Pavlova, everyone examines this document—ragged and burned around the edges—but Dogg, any way you look at it, doesn't resemble Vira Naumivna Pavlova, they also look in the files just in case and discover with astonishment that, according to their records, this same Vira Naumivna passed away three and a half years ago, but things like this occur with their files, says the senior nurse on duty, she refuses wholly to believe that this is not Vira Naumivna who is before her but some unidentified scum, so in the morning they call out the ambulance driver, who celebrated the end of his shift by boozing all night, at first he doesn't understand about Dogg, and says that he never picked up a Vira Naumivna at the stadium yesterday, swears that he is married and that he and his wife get on fine, they even have sex sometimes when he isn't on duty, but, then, in the end he understands what they are talking about and gives the nurses the sergeant's phone number, the one who was interested in Dogg's fate. The nurses rush to telephone the sergeant, saying, as it were, we have a problem, comrade sergeant, there's a piece of trash lying here covered in barf; who do you say is there? asks the sergeant with an early morning zest in his voice and begins immediately to note something down, I am taking notes, he says: co-ver-ed–in–barf, and then what? worse than just covered in barf, say the nurses, he doesn't have a passport, yes-yes-yes, replies the sergeant, not so fast: worse–than–co-ver-ed–in, listen, he suddenly asks, it's not my job, is it? maybe he has suffered a concussion? no—say the nurses—he doesn't have a concussion, or a brain, he's some kind of deserter with someone else's documents, ah-hah, rejoices the sergeant, yes, with someone else's documents and also he has barfed all over everything here—the nurses repeat, unable to calm down, well okay, says the sergeant, drag him over here to us, but quickly, my shift ends at nine, and my partner likely won't have anything to do with him—he has high blood pressure. Of course, say the nurses, high blood pressure.

They immediately call out the driver on duty, take away this rubbish, they say, that has barfed over everything and take him to the district police station, there's something wrong with his documents, uh-huh, says the driver, just like that I'm supposed to drop everything and take this trash somewhere to put his documents in order, maybe even take him to the civil registry office? I don't have anything better to do—in fact he has only just started his shift and really doesn't have anything to do, alright stop making an ass of yourself, says the senior nurse on duty, whose shift is just ending, you'll drive him and come right back, we still have a sea of work, yeah, says the driver, the Black Sea, and squeamishly taking the weakened and demoralized Dogg under his arm he leads him downstairs, opens the emergency vehicle's back doors, come on, he tells Dogg, climb in, sit on the stretcher, or better still lie down, or you'll fall on a turn and break some glass, or cut yourself, or turn over the paint, what paint? asks Dogg, any kind, says the driver, go on, lie down, maybe I should sit? asks Dogg anxiously, don't screw around, says the driver to him and gets behind the wheel. Dogg tries to lie down but immediately feels nauseous and begins to barf—over the stretcher, the walls, some paint, well, you know what I mean. The driver brakes in despair, runs to the back, opens the doors, receives his portion of Dogg's barf, and throws the half-cold Dogg onto Kharkiv's early-morning asphalt, and cursing everything in the world he returns to the hospital, where no one in particular, to be absolutely honest, is waiting for him.

## INTRODUCTION NO. 2

*9.00*

"You know, the worst is that I didn't know there were two of them. One was on the balcony."

"So?"

"So, I entered and she's there alone. I didn't know, you see? And she's lying almost totally naked, next to some panties and bras."

"What, several bras?"

"No, just various sorts of underwear."

"What do you mean?"

"Various colors, you know?"

"I don't even want to talk about it."

"That's my point. I don't like underwear in general. Women's underwear, that is."

"Well, sure."

"In short, I see that she's pissed, and start taking off my own clothes. I didn't know they'd been at it since that morning, you know, first swallowed some junk, then chased it down with vodka, just imagine? Drunken bitches. And I'm standing there with an erection."

"Amazing."

"And then the bitch, the second one, comes in from the balcony. And of course gets frightened."

"Naturally…"

"The one in the room is okay, she's used to it, probably."

"To what?"

"To me. She's already seen me like that, you know, with an erection."

"Unbelievable."

"That's what I'm saying. But the other, the one on the balcony, is completely soused, you see, they'd been drinking since morning, the bitches. You get the picture?"

"Yeah, broads. I have a neighbor. He goes out and buys two liters of vodka every morning."

"Two liters?"

"Seriously."

"I feel bad just thinking about it."

"I ask him: man, why the fuck do you need two liters? You won't be able to drink it all. And you know what he says?"

"What?"

"After I finish the first bottle, I'm afraid to go out anywhere. But I still want to drink, I can't stop myself."

"Seriously?"

"What the hell is he afraid of?"

"Well, I don't know, he's terrified. He starts to get this terror after drinking vodka. But he still wants to drink. So he takes two liters right away. Sits and gets pickled."

"Hang on, he downs one container then the second—hell, he finishes drinking it all. Then what?"

"What do you mean, then what?"

"He still wants to drink?"

"Yeah."

"But he's afraid to go out?"

"No, no way, they have this system, you see: when he finishes off two liters—"

"Two liters!"

"—right, two liters—some switch gets flipped and he's not afraid anymore."

"Seriously?"

"I saw it myself."

"Well, how does he feel?"

"What do you mean?"

"How does he feel if he's not afraid?"

"He doesn't give a damn."

"And so then what?"

"And he takes off for more vodka. He's stambling, but off he goes."

"Yeah…"

"To get more."

"And you say—an erection."

"What erection?"

"You were saying—an erection."

"Well, yes, an erection."

"And then what?"

"Nothing. I'm standing there with my erection."

"Unbelievable…"

"And then?"

"Then this drunken bitch walks in off the balcony, can you imagine?"

"I can't imagine it."

"Well, she sees me, and, you know, thinks—who is this moron, and why is he just standing there?"

"What's standing?"

"Standing, she says to herself. She's thinking: probably a neighbor come to get laid. And so she grabs an empty champagne bottle and fires it into my skull."

"And you?"

"Well, I lost consciousness. I fell down, that is, all covered in blood. And this drunken bitch, just image, runs up to the other one and starts to wake her, get up, she says, we have to tie him up—meaning me. She gets up and on top of everything they take the bedsheets and tie up my arms and legs."

"But they knew you, at least the other one did."

"Yeah, but they were both pissed since morning, the bitches, that's what I'm saying! They ate some junk, and then drank vodka. How that bitch made it back from the balcony I don't know. They could barely recognize one another."

"And then?"

"So they tie me up and drag me to the bath, throw me in, and go to sleep."

"Yeah—"

"And so in the morning one of them, the one who came from the balcony, naturally she has forgotten everything, and makes for the bath to wash. Besides, the beast doesn't switch the light on but gropes her way in. She climbs into the tub, and there I am..."

"Vodka, you know, it jams a woman's signals, they become like fish."

"I once met a ticket controller in a streetcar, she was going around with her ticket punch."

"Don't bullshit."

"What bullshit? Seriously, the broad was going about completely drunk, I give her my ticket and she pulls out a punch from her pocket, can you imagine?"

"Must be cool to have your own ticket validator."

"Exactly."

"Yeah..."

"I tried to rip one out of a streetcar once. I was traveling at night, there was no one else, so I start to break it off, cut my hand open, can you believe it, blood's flowing everywhere, and then the controllers come in."

"Bitches."

"They went straight for me, I was basically the only passenger, there was no one else. Why the hell are you breaking the validator?"

"And what did you say?"

"Me? I said I'm not breaking anything, I wanted to punch my ticket and your fucking machine chewed up my hand. Here, look, I say."

"Cool."

"Yeah…"

Cocoa, sluggish and sweaty, feels pretty good in this company. The little room in which they sit is full of smoke and smells of coffee, there are not enough cups for everyone, they pass the first coffee around, then the second, transferring the cup from hand to hand, then they pass around pieces of white bread, after an hour spent in the room their clothes and hair and they themselves smell of tobacco and bread, even more of bread. Cocoa wipes the sweat off his brow with his sleeve, what's with you, Cocoa, they all laugh, that's your best suit, no trouble, Cocoa blushes, don't worry, I'll wash it, well yeah, they continue to laugh, you've promised to do that for over a year, take some bread, Cocoa takes some fresh white bread from the hands of his friends and continues to listen to the stories, he'd gladly spend all his time with them, he feels good with them, they share their bread and cigarettes with him, and the main thing is no one drives him away. Try in our day to find a group ready to put up for a few days with you and your sand-colored suit that hasn't been washed in over a year, or maybe two.

Cocoa is a bit too plump for this company, and in his suit he looks terrible, but he likes it—I don't even know where they sell that kind. Anyway, Cocoa found it somewhere, considers it stylish, he's up on such things, he's practically the only one of my acquaintances who goes to the hairdresser, uses some kind of gay gel, even shaves from time to time though this doesn't help. Six of them are in the room, sitting and listening to Little Chuck Berry, who has just explained how he celebrated his birthday, everyone liked the story, Cocoa listened with his mouth wide open; he especially liked the part about the underwear in various colors, and tries to imagine this but cannot. In the meantime Little Chuck Berry passes another cigarette around and suddenly says, Cocoa, tell us something, and everyone agrees, yeah Cocoa, come on, tell us something, how come you just sit there silently, we're interested, come on, tell us something, know what—tell us about your babes, everyone laughs, yeah, they say, Cocoa, come on, tell us about your babes. Cocoa looks embarrassed, he doesn't feel completely sure of himself after all, they're a team and he's just a visitor, but he doesn't want to leave, so he thinks about what he could say that it would be about women. About women. Most of the women he sees are on TV. Maybe he should tell them about television.

One of the event organizers rushes into the room, that's enough, he shouts, come on, come on, quickly, it's time to begin, and they begin to get up and they slide into the corridor walking in a line, one after the other, still munching their bread, finishing their cigarettes, Cocoa follows them, they go through some back alleys, everywhere there are banners with slogans and fire extinguishers on the walls, finally they come out into the light, someone turns to Cocoa and says: alright, pal, wait for us here, okay? we won't be long. How long is this going to take? asks Cocoa; a couple of hours, maybe a bit longer, come on, sit down there by the wall and wait. Can I listen? asks Cocoa. Okay listen, says someone, listen, but really it isn't very interesting—in fact its total bullshit. Cocoa can do nothing but take them at their word.

The hall is packed, more than two thousand people have gathered, latecomers are standing in the aisles, pushing and shoving each other up by the stage, the public is freaky: students, pensioners, military, invalids, yes, a lot of invalids, although this is understandable; there are even businessmen wearing suits in harsh colors, and so on. When they appear the hall erupts joyfully, the invalids begin to chant their mantras, they wave their arms at them, smile, even a few bouquets go flying on stage, they come out and unhurriedly pick up their instruments, plug them in, one of them gives a signal to the sound engineers, as though saying more of me, another opens a bottle of water, the crowd continues to chant, creating a celebration, but they don't get into it too much, everyone knows what is happening, who the main attraction really is and how everything is going to end, and when the pumped-up invalids begin to sing in chorus almost no one pays attention, and then, he arrives—

*10.00*

His reverence Johnson-and-Johnson, sun on the beclouded horizon of American evangelism, star of the biggest mass euphorias on the West coast, leader of the Church of Jesus (United), the pop-star who works the minds of all who desire it and who have come to him on this rainy summer morning in mid-week, his reverence Johnson-and–Johnson doesn't give a damn about all these silly conventions, he's not some Old Believer who only holds services on weekends, what crap, he says, what old-style crap, and everyone agrees with him. He arrived in town a couple of weeks ago, at least that's what's written in the press releases that are being handed to everyone who enters, the concert hall was booked a month in advance, he hired some musicians and now is the third day of his screwing around here preaching God's word to the aboriginals, each day there are more of these aboriginals, his reverence has great PR agents, all the city's newspapers began writing about his arrival a month ago, leaflets with his smiling American mug were distributed at factories, market-places, and banks, on the first day of his arrival he was interviewed on the most popular TV station, and to the great amazement of the viewing public spoke the state language more-or-less respectably, scoring big points from the first moment, he said that he had local roots but in general was a WASP, meaning a hundred-percent white from Texas, not surprisingly the entire city discussed his reverence, during the first sermon there were several television cameras in the hall, all the news channels considered it appropriate to announce that the first sermon of his reverence Johnson-and-Johnson, whom the Bolsheviks had spoken about for so long, had taken place, everything was cool and, dear Kharkivites, you simply have to see this, all the more so because admission is free and everyone gets a free calendar with a glossy color photograph of his reverence: services will be held every day at ten, thirteen, and seventeen hundred hours, seven days a week, until the end of June.

And so this is the fourth day in a row that he's raking in the money preaching three sermons a day, he already has fans here who react devotedly to his reverence's every runny-nosed sob, translated for them by some dame in a gray business suit who works as his reverence's interpreter and apparently doesn't understand him, in any case she translates haphazardly, and his reverence himself obviously can't be bothered to correct her, God's revelations obviously affect his mind, he simply gets high during the sermon, even dope smokers have started to come, they understand the old guy in their own way, showing some sort of universal solidarity among all stoned idiots who in one way or another, each in his own way, of course, are discovering God's secrets—they're all feeling a buzz together now, and there's music playing too.

They're the ones playing the music, in casting his reverence screened them carefully, choosing mainly students of the conservatory, with only Little Chuck Berry coming from the punks, his reverence took him because of his sense of rhythm, overall education was not a deciding factor, the main thing was to look good on stage, and, naturally, no Jews, no Mongols, absolutely no blacks—in a word, real fascist scum, but the people like it.

His reverence gets himself psyched-up in the dressing room, swallows some kind of pills, drinks a lot of decaf coffee, and loudly recites something from De Holy Bible, telling the interpreter to repeat after him, the interpreter stays darkly silent, which winds up his reverence even more, he begins to show the first signs of God's revelation, which with him is like diarrhea, he just bursts and it's all there. One of the organizers comes in, it's time, time to go on, the crowd is waiting, his reverence sips his low octane coffee from a big plastic mug, spills some on his snow-white shirt, shit, he says, fucking shit, the interpreter attempts to translate this for the doofus organizer, but he just waves her off. Fine, says his reverence, I'll have to button up completely, like an oyster or mollusk, like an octopus—in a word, we all walk in God's sight, he adds, and goes out into the corridor. In the wings, under the stage itself, his reverence stops for a moment, his attention is drawn to a plump young man in a sand-colored suit, just a regular kid, thinks his reverence and slows down for a moment. Who are you? he asks and the backstage shadows are suddenly illuminated by the gleam of his wristwatch. Cocoa freezes and momentarily loses the gift of speech, why don't you talk? says his reverence impatiently, do you have a name? Cocoa nods his large head but doesn't give his name. Well, fine, his reverence loses what remains of his patience, may the Lord's great mercy lie on jerks like you too, the interpreter wants to translate this, but his reverence interrupts her—later, later, he says, and goes on stage, dragging with difficulty the eternally-lit yellow halo above his head.

Cocoa, his eyes popping out, stares at the spot where his reverence just stood, takes a long time to return to consciousness, and his shaky legs carry him along as he looks for the toilet, finally he finds it, uses his remaining strength to open the door, creep inside, and begins to throw up. I noticed a long time ago that when he gets nervous, when he's stressed out or something, he always throws up, he just can't help it, whenever a new session begins its better to stay away from him, that's the kind of guy he is. "Lord," says Cocoa, "Oh, Lord, is this really me, is it really me whom this man just approached? It cannot be—I know my own worth, I have nice friends, my mother works in the library, they know me fairly well in Makivka and in Milove, but something like this! I don't even know what to think," he thinks and begins to throw up again. "How can it be," he thinks after throwing up, "no one will believe me. They will say you're making it up. Christ, I don't believe it myself. I live like everybody else, do my work honestly, don't get in anyone's way, don't try to mess anybody up, maybe this is God's thanks. Otherwise how —I just don't understand—how could it happen that I, me alone, was approached, just like that, by a man WITH A GOLD-PLATED ROLEX ON HIS WRIST!!!"

Cocoa leans down once more and sees down on the floor by the sink a pile of brochures with his reverence's sermons, he devoutly takes one, examines the slightly crumpled face of Johnson-and-Johnson, examines the rolex on his wrist, and, smiling, hides the brochure in the pocket of his sand-colored jacket.

My dear brothers and sisters! (Dear brothers and sisters! translates the dame in the gray suit.) Through the manipulation of his divine hands the Lord has gathered us here together! (The Lord has made certain manipulations, she translates. A whole pile of them.) So let us thank him for gathering us—you and I—together! (So thank you for gathering here, and myself.) I tell you, brothers and sisters: let us rise, let us rise and pray, in the name of the father, Hallelujah! (Alleluia! says the dame, not quite understanding him.) Lord, I say! (He says

"Lord.") Look upon these people who have gathered here this morning! (They gathered early this morning.) Your divine love has brought them here, hasn't it?" (Love hasn't brought them here.) Yes, Lord! (Yes.) Yes, Hallelujah! (The dame remains silent.) But you might ask why are you, his reverence Johnson-and-Johnson, talking to us about this, we know all this about ourselves, so you better show us a miracle! (We know everything about you! says the dame threateningly. Just ask.)

I want to tell you a story, I want to show you a concrete example, so that you might understand what I have in mind. (For example, I want to show you—you understand what I have in mind.) A girl from southern Connecticut (A girl from the South) lived in great hardship (lived in the South), she had no parents, no friends, no personal psychologist (she practiced psychology, she was a psychologist, her own), she lost all hope of God's revelation, and her days dragged on in an endless stream (she lost everything and threw herself around endlessly). Hallelujah! (The dame remains silent.) One day she came upon a man of God, a clergyman (a man appeared in her life, a male) and he said to her "Sister!" (she was his sister) "Sister!" (another one), abandon this nightmare, you yourself are closing the door through which Jesus could enter your life (close the door, he said, the nightmarish Dzhizus might come). Wherefore do you do this? (Where are you doing this?) And he left her, he had enough of her faithlessness (The old man, it appears, had had her and he had enough of her and left). And she was left all alone, and her days continued to drag on in an endless stream (And she continued to drag herself around all alone) and then once, when she was returning after buying some things (Once, she finally made it out shopping) and was crossing the street, some drunken car enthusiast couldn't stop in time and knocked her down (she was so drunk, she could not stop herself and fell down like a racing groupie), and when she woke up in a trauma unit on the operating table (she woke up on a table, you know, drunk, dirty, in torn clothing, just another hooker) under the surgeon's scalpel (the surgeon was on top of her), she could not remember her name (she could not even remember him. Yes, she forgot everything, she was a lush, a total alcoholic), she had lost her memory! She remembered nothing (she had boozed away everything: her house and things, she emptied her bank account and squandered that too, she found a squeeze and they began to make moonshine), she could not remember where she had come from (where did she come from? worried the neighbors), she could not remember her parents, her father, her mother (your mother, they said, this whore has moved into our building, they'll soon switch off our electricity because of her unpaid bills), she forgot her whole life (we've been working hard all our lives, and then this slut comes along and settles into a cushy easy life and even brings a squeeze along with her), and when everyone, even the doctors, had lost faith (you bitch, we'll show you how we maintain exemplary living standards and the moral code of the builders of communism in our building. We'll rip your legs off, you low-life. And we'll have your squeeze committed to the detox center for treatment), God's revelation was suddenly upon her (because you've turned into a brazen hussy, you railway-station bitch with your squeeze, you whore, you think that we're going to pay for your electricity, that you're the smartest one on the block, you sea slime with your fucked-up joke of a squeeze, we'll lock him up in rehab for good, no more pandering to that shithead, we'll call the district cop right away, we'll cut off your electricity and we'll circumcise your pimp too, that sailor of the merchant marine, the screwed-up comedian, settling down into the cushy, easy life, what a whore, the tart), and God said to her (fuck off, girlie, get your ass off the beach, we've worked here all our lives and you think what? you think you're number one? you want to hide behind your squeeze, your sailor? The detox lock-up is just crying out for your sailor, you see, yes, the detox). What detox? Johnson-and-Johnson suddenly thinks, what is this fucking bitch translating? He pauses, during which time the weeping of invalids can be heard, then he continues.

Dear brothers and sisters! (Dear brothers and sisters! the interpreter returns closer to the topic.) The Lord said to her: reflect on everything that has happened (the Lord says to you: reflect what's happening!), get up and go! (Leave!), and she went (and she left), and she asked the doctors (ask the doctors): who paid for my treatment? (who's going to pay for everything). And they told her: it's a miracle, the Lord's miracle, but someone paid for your insurance (buy insurance for your little miracle), and someone gave you some clothing and things—that's a second miracle (another thing, someone donated a miracle for you), and someone has rented an apartment for you, you now have a roof over your head, and that's a third miracle (and this miracle is now over your head for the third time). And then she understood: this was the Lord's revelation, a revelation that revealed itself to her (and then she had a revelation), and that Jesus himself was granting her a light, a small one, a small ray of light, like when you open the fridge at night (the nightmarish Dzhizus wants to give her a fridge at night, just a small one). Why must I tell you this, brothers and sisters? (What are you expecting, brothers and sisters?) So that you might understand that the Lord's revelation is like products of the sea (the exhausted dame falls into silence, lost in thought), the main thing is not just knowing how to catch them, the main thing is knowing how to prepare them. The Lord's revelation is like the brain of an octopus: you don't know where to look for it. Because when you walk up to an octopus and look at it you think: Hallelujah! where is this fucking octopus's brain? After all, an octopus must have a brain! But your mind cannot resolve this, your mind is lazy and disillusioned, you cannot simply pick up the octopus and do your thing, you have to consult your inner voice, which tells you "Drop it, drop it, you don't know anything about this, this task is beyond you." And then you begin to doubt yourself. Hallelujah! You think: yes, I am not worthy of this, I am too weak and frail to walk this path to the end and to figure everything out, this is not a job for me. I would rather stand aside. Because when you see his body, it's the same as your body; and his eyes, they're the same as your eyes; and when you hear his heart beat—praise the Lord—it beats just like yours! And who are you?

"An octopus!" shouts someone in the hall.

"What octopus?" Johnson-and-Johnson is confused, why an octopus? he pauses for a moment, nonplussed, but he doesn't miss the wave and once more dives into the colorful purple sermonizing shit: correct, you are a child of God! We are all God's children! The Lord's revelation is in all of us (Every one of us, joins in the dame, will receive on the way out a brochure and small calendar with his reverence's photo), so let us heed the attention of the almighty (thank you for your attention, all the best, until we meet again at the next sermons of the Church of Jesus (United)), with whom we must meet! (until we meet again, the dame repeats. Don't forget your things, she adds, and get those fucking invalids out of here).

I certainly put on a show, didn't I, says his reverence Johnson-and-Johnson to the doofus organizer. The doofus looks at him with the eyes of a man in love. Yeah, repeats his reverence, I certainly showed them. Only why did I get into the octopus thing again, what is it with me in the last while? he asks the doofus, the moment I take vitamins I start talking about octopuses. I just can't stop myself, he offers in justification, these enchanting creatures turn me on. Oh, how they turn me on, he says joyfully and disappears into his dressing room.

*11.00*

While all these orthodox believers in the seventh day are still leaving and his reverence, waving his arms, is quitting the stage, Cocoa stays seated on a bench trying to understand what they are talking about, but he has trouble making sense of his reverence's speech, something about electricity and a detox centre, about octopuses. Cocoa is bored, I should have stayed at home and watched television, he thinks, but here in addition to his reverence's revelations, reinforcing the drama of the agitational work among the aboriginals, the "Divine Orchestra of His Reverence Johnson-and-Johnson" begins to play—these are Cocoa's friends, cannon fodder in the decisive stage of the unequal battle between good and evil and his reverence Johnson-and-Johnson's with his own mental enfeeblement. They play blues, some classical pieces selected personally by the boss for them, the invalids in the hall begin to rock in tune, the businessmen unbutton their lettuce-colored jackets, the public livens up, in his dressing room his reverence joyfully wipes the sweat from his face, his rolex flashes, the band gets into its number, they are playing an old theme but gradually moving away from it, then finally letting loose with something they were definitely not taught in the conservatory: "Atomic Bomb Blues," written in the distant postwar years by Homer Harris, who is unknown to anyone here, even to his reverence Johnson-and-Johnson, whose divine revelation does not find its way into such borderline territory, how could that fucking octopus know about Homer Harris. Cocoa likes this considerably more than his reverence's sermons, he understands everything, he begins to rock in tune with the music behind the stage and suddenly hears someone in the band take off, cutting right across the musical score, Cocoa immediately recognizes the guitar of Little Chuck Berry, who has obviously also caught hold of his revelation and seems to be saying to the crowd of invalids:

Lord, if you can hear me beyond the cries of this beast Johnson-and-Johnson, if you have not totally given up participating in all this, give me a chance, just a few sentences, that is all, and I will quickly explain things to you, the main thing is give me your attention, I am after all playing in the divine orchestra, even if I am complete shit in your eyes and an embarrassment to look at because of everything that I, as it were, do, don't turn away from me for a few seconds more, I feel terrible, God, how terrible I feel no one can know, and I play terribly, but all the same send me just a little ray of light, if I am expressing myself understandably, shake up this sadness in my lungs, in my heart and stomach, all this shit, so-to-speak, do you hear, I am asking only for a little light, I'm only 19, maybe I have waited a very short time, but I am only asking for a small ray of light, a tiny one, the kind you get at night when you open the fridge, you know what I'm talking about, so that I might breathe out all that I have breathed in during those 19 years, just a little joy, God, a minimal amount, don't go to any special trouble, just when you have the chance, hear me, anything at all, just a bit, anything at all, any kind of revelation, do you hear, God, okay? Okay? and some sneakers, God, sneakers, a pair of sneakers, do you hear?! do you hear me?!! you, do you hear, do you hear anything I am saying?!!! hey??!!!!! hey?!!! he-e-e-e-e-y!!!!!!!!!! he-e-e-e-e-e-e-e-e-e-e-e-e-e-e-e-e-e-e-e-e-e-e-e-e-e-e-e-e-ey!!!!!!!!!!!!!

The band picks up this whimsical theme, they all immediately get what a cool guy this Little Chuck Berry is, how neatly he has put it all together, so they each try not to spoil anything, Cocoa had not heard anything this good for a long time, he simply collapsed onto the bench, sat there motionless and listened, listened, while they poured it on and poured it on, and even when the invalids began slithering away, and the businessmen wandered off to their cabs, and the cleaning ladies began going through the rows to collect the empty vodka bottles and the crumpled little calendars with his reverence's American mug, they still could not stop. How they played! Like gods! That is, they were hardly faking it at all.

## INTRODUCTION NO. 3

*00.00*

My friends want to be taken seriously. They are very sensitive about how people speak to them and about what, and how people look at them, they try to understand what others are thinking about them while talking, they are always causing scandals, it's hard to have a conversation with them, they get nervous among strangers, from time from time they are thrown out of somewhere, if one of them were to fly in a plane he'd be thrown out of that too, no doubt about it. I used to find all this okay but lately I've started to get upset too. I don't like it, for example, when someone forgets my name, let's say we are talking away and suddenly it becomes clear that no one knows what my name is, there are so many jack-asses around; and another thing I can't stand is when someone has some kind of shit on their face, I'm not talking about them being a one-eyed Cyclops, of course, but about them maybe having cut themselves in shaving, or having blood on their lips or something—I don't like it, to my mind it shows disrespect, to walk around with that kind of crap on your face, if you don't know how to shave then stay home, stare at the television or take up something useful, but no, they have to mess up their mug with some razor and then go meet you on the street and start loading you up with totally useless stuff without even remembering your name, on top of everything. And another thing, I don't like cosmetics, they're terrible things, cosmetics, they're aggressive and smell awful, I can't stand perfumes, I can understand drinking them but in general I don't see it, and various rings, earings, badges—all of these show disrespect, at least that's how I see it. None of this used to bother me—

generally speaking, in the past I just didn't notice a lot of things, life is such a cool thing, but the further you sail into its ocean the more shit there is floating around you, floating without sinking, but on the other hand that also makes it more interesting.

I have quite a few friends, you can't really call us a group, we're more a kind of friendly collection of con-men out to sucker every recruiter and employer, we live in several adjoining rooms on the same floor, sleep wherever there's room, I don't even know everyone, there's only one real friend here—Vasia the Communist—the rest are more or less transients, although they're also our friends, they appear and disappear, sometimes there can be up to ten of them on our floor, at other times I wander around the corridors by myself for days, climb onto the roof and look around. We are all 18 or 19, most of my friends have been thrown out of school, they are now either unemployed or spend their time doing useless things, Dogg Pavlov for example, I never could understand what he really did. Dogg Pavlov's parents are Jews, but he doesn't transfer that on to himself, he says that parents are parents and kids are kids, he is himself; moreover, Dogg Pavlov says that he's right. Consequently, he doesn't live with his parents, says he cannot live with Jews, hangs around acquaintances, sometimes hangs with us for a week or two, he has a granny too, who's obviously not Jewish, because he sometimes stays with her. From time to time he steals pieces of antique porcelain from his granny's buffet and sells them at the flea market, using the money to buy pills in the pharmacy kiosks near the market and then comes over to our place. Then we don't even leave the room for several days, except maybe to take a leak or to puke—but you can puke in the room, too. You can piss too, come to think of it. I like Dogg Pavlov, even in spite of his anti-Semitism, it doesn't affect me.

It's against Dogg's principles to work, he considers it degrading, "it's degrading to work for them," he says.

In general he believes that there's been a putsch in our republic and that the Jews have come to power, yids, he says, there are yids everywhere; I myself think he's wrong, but I don't want to work either. Recently, it's true, our friends the advertisers Vova and Volodia set Dogg up with a job as a courier in their newspaper in the advertising section, Dogg struggled with this for a long time, came to visit us on the floor, wandered around the kitchen, called Vova and Volodia Jews, and vacillated. In the end he plucked up the courage and went to work. He worked for about ten days. Then he disappeared for about ten days, along with some correspondence, Vova and Volodia came to see us but we knew nothing, they phoned his parents, they too hadn't heard anything from their son Dogg for about six months, which apparently suited them fine, the boys even went to visit the granny, she didn't let them in, granny looked at them through the half-open door and didn't understand what they wanted from her, it seems Dogg has finally driven the old woman nuts, try living with a grandson who starts breakfast by drinking vodka and then has everything else. In a word Dogg disappeared and our friends the advertisers threatened to do something terrible to him if he was ever found—"pass on the message to Dogg," they told us, "that we will tear his balls off." I doubted that Dogg could be enticed back to the editorial office this way, but I promised to pass on the message. It wasn't hard for me to do. We didn't like Vova and Volodia too much, but we put up with them, they studied in the history department and, like most of the A students in the history department, they worked for the KGB; the KGB, I think, suffered a lot from the presence in its ranks of two dolts like Vova and Volodia, but order is order, that's what I think, why else would they keep them on staff. Vova and Volodia, obviously with the protection of the KGB, in their first year of studies set themselves up at the advertising agency of one of Kharkiv's first independent newspapers, their newspaper received money from some democratic development fund, the editor was some slimy prick who had been able to get a big grant from the Yanks and they began putting out their independent newspaper, they were one of the first in the city to start printing naked babes on the front cover, and detailed television listings in the centerfold. In addition they constantly attacked our USSR, one might say that using Yankee money they poured shit on our Soviet fatherland, on the days of our youth, so-to-speak, I didn't like the newspaper, though I liked the babes on the front cover. Vova and Volodia worked, as I said, in the advertising department, I don't know how well, probably badly, because they began dropping in on us once or twice a week, drinking vodka and fighting with each other. Generally speaking they were pals and got on well together. Vova was a bit taller, Volodia a bit heavier, but when they got drunk they would go out unnoticed into the corridor and start bashing each other, for real, no fooling around, with teeth knocked-out, snot and tears running down their faces. So what kind of KGB agents they were, I can't say. At first we would pull them apart, then we realized it was no use, if the fellas want to fight, let them fight. Maybe that's normal among historians, maybe the KGB pays them extra for it, who cares.

And then there's Vakha, who also lives on the floor with us. Vakha's a Georgian, although Dogg calls him a Jew too. Vakha has his own business, near the ring-road just by the exit from the city, quite near us, he has several kiosks in which several vendors work. The vendors live in one of the kiosks, get together for the night, in winter they make a fire, once they almost burned down the kiosk, thank God it was made of steel and they only got roasted a bit but survived. Vakha has two whole rooms. He lives in one himself and keeps his smuggled goods in the other one—various chocolates, colas, heroin, and other lollipops. He pays off the cops, the guards too, but he leaves us alone, so Vakha is a positive hero, completely positive, there's no other word for it. He sells us undiluted vodka but doesn't give us any discount. Vakha is afraid of Dogg, and whenever the latter comes to see us he locks himself up in one of the rooms; at these times I imagine him counting his worn-out banknotes and swallowing gold coins to prevent Dogg, the anti-Semitic Jew, from taking any of it away.

Further down the corridor, somewhere in its depth lives Cocoa the Donbas intellectual. That is, his mother works in the library of one of the mines. Cocoa is portly and we don't like him, but he's still drawn to us, well, in general he doesn't really have any alternatives, who's going to spend time with a Donbas intellectual. Although he does have some other acquaintances in the city besides us, some musicians, obviously dandies like Cocoa, and after visiting them he crawls home on all fours completely plastered on port wine, and collapses into sleep. Cocoa has a sand-colored suit in which he looks like a total nerd, he just about never takes it off, almost takes it into the shower with him too; when he fills himself with port wine he falls into bed in this suit, it turns out to be a multi-functional thing, this costume of a Donbas intellectual. When he wakes up, Cocoa comes to the kitchen and observes who is preparing what, sniffs the processed foods, and chats about various subjects—sober, portly, in his crumpled dandy costume.

Further down the corridor, somewhere in that labyrinth, lives Sailor, a solitary guy with a torn right ear, he says that a dog bit it off—Pavlov? someone is always sure to ask by way of a joke. Sailor is either God-fearing or maybe just a bit nerdy, I don't even know how to explain it, for example he only washes at night, says he doesn't want to be disturbed—disturbed from doing what? I ask him all the time, Sailor blushes but continues to wash only at night, that's how he is.

Among the others one could perhaps mention Carburetor, that's right, Sasha Carburetor, my good friend,

Sasha arrived from some place along the border, though this border is everywhere around us, Sasha in fact came in defiance of his parents' wishes, it turns out that such things do indeed happen, his mother and stepfather are still at home; Sasha finished driver education courses, has a real driver's license, and hopes to start a trucking operation some day, to buy a hearse or something and to transport, say, furniture, he's passionate about technology, if you understand what I mean. One time he even bought himself a textbook with diagrams and descriptions of automobiles and tried to make sense of it all. He began, as you can probably guess, with the carburetor. After this the textbooks disappeared, I figure someone just sold them for alcohol, why not put them to good use. Overall, Carburetor has this capacity for stepping into shit that isn't meant for him.

As for the others, I don't even know them very well myself, various comic book heroes appear from time to time, but to keep track of them all and why they have appeared in our lives is pretty hard to do. Let's say some Ivanenko appears, a curious type, not to say fucked-up, and basically, that's about all that can be said about him. That's all there is.

A nice, eternally hungry crew, held together by no one knows what, because in principle everyone has issues with everyone else, but this is still no reason to avoid healthy interaction. We have nothing to do for the most part, although everyone has his own relations with reality, at our age these come down to some sort of simple whims and desires—to get laid, or something, I don't know what else there is. Women ignore us, even the prostitutes on the ring-road, we occasionally go over to look at the prostitutes, sort of an excursion to see the free attractions, of course we have no money, so we just hang out with them, bum some cigarettes, share various life stories, in a word we get in their way while they're trying to earn prostitution's hard bread. However, they treat us well, out there on the ring-road they're not particularly useful to anybody, just like us, and just like us they don't have enough money or societal love, both they and we have to live through the torrents of rain this summer in an empty Kharkiv suburb overgrown with grass and plastered with advertisements, this fantastic city, these fantastic prostitutes, this fantastic life. We don't practice homosexuality, though everything is leading us in that direction.

*7.00*

The main thing is to count everything correctly, in this kind of thing if you don't think everything through you'll fall on your face, nothing is as simple as it looks when you start your own business, start to sell something, you have to give it some thought, even if you're dealing with what seems to be an absolute winner of a deal it's best to insure yourself. It's one thing if, for instance, you're dealing with stocks or transfers, in a word if the bucks are not in your hands, someone else can count things up for you, you only have to do what is required of you and not spend time shitting around while on the job. It's a completely different thing if you're working with real live cash, man, with a wad of bills, and there's no office to back you up, when you're face to face—no middlemen—with a living, breathing pile of money, that's when you'd better think things through, or you'll end up screwed, no two ways about it. How many times have I seen otherwise normal people grasp at some obviously losing proposition and then predictably flame out, losing the balance of their financial resources and their social respectability—the average business is so dangerous that even one false step and right away you have a soldering iron up your ass, that's what the primitive accumulation of capital is like in the conditions of a post-totalitarian society.

At first they offered me a piece of the action too, but for some reason I refused, I don't know why, something made me suspicious, I can't even say what—they looked completely serious, my friend Vasia the Communist, a nice guy, an exceptional carefree spirit, suddenly had enough of living on vodka with tea, with constant shortages, added everything up and reached the conclusion that the situation was difficult; the four of them decided to pool their resources, travel to Russia, buy two crates of vodka with all their dollars—buying dollars here and exchanging them in Russia would net them a profit, especially if they worked on a big scale, well two crates is no big scale, but who cares. They were going to travel to Russia and back on the suburban trains, to save money on transport, on the way they would live off the same vodka, they would bring it back and turn it over for double what they paid, then they would travel to Russia again and buy four crates of vodka, bring it back the same way and turn it over the same way, this would take some time but with a couple of nights at Kharkiv's South Station you could sell anything, even your soul, if you had one, and then the most interesting part would begin—they would travel one more time, the last, and with all their dollars would buy eight crates of vodka, transporting it would be a bit riskier, but it was worth a try, if anything happened they would be able to buy off the customs officials with the very same vodka, though that would be a shame.

So, they said to me, we end up with two crates of vodka per mug, can you imagine? Well, I say, and so what? And then, they said with emphasis on the fricative, we guzzle it all!!! What, all eight crates? Yes! We won't be able to do it, I say. Fuck, says Vasia the Communist, in about three days we will, for sure. I imagined those three days and turned down the offer.

Vasia really knows how to make this kind of thing work, I understand him in principle, he has nothing to lose, this is his chance to have at least a few days without shortages in his food basket, which in his case consists almost exclusively of various liquor and vodka products, actually vodka, what does liquor have to do with it. He collects his boy scouts, convinces Sailor, Sailor agrees pretty quickly—why not make the trip, he says, there's nothing for him to do in the city, even the police are not interested in him, because Sailor is living here without official registration, as one would expect from a sea wolf—during the nights he hides in the shower, during the day he sleeps it off, very few people know about his existence, like a soldier waiting for his discharge, in short, they attract a couple more young guys of uncertain social origins and formal status, Vasia conducts agitational work among them all Wednesday night to Thursday, saying that in Russia you can now buy almost anything for a song, you can even buy a tank and drive it across the border, but they don't want tanks, they want vodka, so the plan appeals to everyone, I would have agreed too, as I already said, but it didn't work out. And so in the morning they get up early to travel in search of their illusory bluebirds of happiness, alcohol at discount prices, they pool whatever money they've got but don't have enough even for an ice cream.

They have to sell something. Someone in the group produces a camera, here's a camera, he says, but won't you regret it? they ask, hah, it's okay, he says, there's nothing to photograph anyway, that's true, everyone agrees, what is there to photograph, Vasia himself finds a pair of forgotten binoculars somewhere, I for one didn't even know he had a pair of binoculars, although we are friends, there's a surprise for you. Well, so now all that's left is for someone to sell all this junk. In principle, thinks Vasia, we could sell it to Sailor, he's a simpleton, he would buy it. But Sailor is part of the group. We could sell it to Cocoa, Cocoa is a simpleton too, and he's not in the group. But Cocoa is not only not in the group, he has completely disappeared, no one has seen him for several days already. And here someone remembers Vakha, right, says Vasia, Vakha's a Georgian, Georgians like optical instruments, don't they? someone in the group asks without confidence, well of course, says Vasia, of course: all Georgians like optical instruments, and they go to Vakha and find him in one of his kiosks, they say something like Vakha, how about buying these optical instruments?

But on this cool June morning Vakha doesn't quite have his head together, he is up to his ears in his own cannabis, which he smokes every evening with his vendors, so Vakha gets scared, what optical instruments, commander? why optical instruments? he asks. Vasia reaches into his bag and pulls out an old pair of binoculars with no straps and an almost unused FED 5 camera in a creaking leather case, here, he says to Vakha, take it, you won't regret it, it's good stuff. Vakha is still frightened and doesn't leave the kiosk, he sits there with his vendors and looks at Vasia through the narrow service window, but Vasia smiles at him in a friendly manner and the rest of the scouts also smile, although a little tensely, and Vakha suddenly thinks, fuck, he thinks, fuck, what am I doing, why am I sitting here, what time is it, who are these morons standing in front of me and, most important, why are they carrying binoculars?!! But voices whisper something to him and in the end he comes out of the kiosk and takes the optical instruments into his disobedient hands, he is led aside, so that he would have something to look at through the binoculars, the street is empty, the air around the kiosks smells of cannabis and rain. Vakha looks into the binoculars and with religious awe observes the full, quiet bus stop, last stop of the No. 38 bus, several prostitutes at the crossroads, and, further along the curve, an unfinished nine-story building whose walls are being built by cons, a dilapadated Soviet-era supermarket, the No. 20 streetcar crawling out of some wetlands, and going full circle around himself in this fashion his optically privileged eye suddenly hits upon a kiosk, his very own, and before his clouded gaze the sign "PRIVATE SHOP VAKHA" suddenly arises with great clarity— not fucking bad, he thinks, that's me, and he ends up completely amazed.

After selling the optical instruments and receiving a pretty good sum, at least as far as their boy scout needs went, right there over the body of the half-conscious Vakha, our friends buy from his vendors two one-liter bottles of Kaiser-brand vodka and travel directly to the railway station to catch the first suburban train of the day to the town of Belgorod, they are somewhat excited and noisy in the fragrant summer morning under the fresh skies, these fearless seekers of joy and adventure, seen from the side they really do look like tourists, or even more like pilgrims on a pilgrimage to the glorious Rus' town of Belgorod and they're not taking along anything superfluous except the two one-liter Kaisers and their student tickets, and bearing in mind that they will drink the Kaisers before getting to Belgorod they really aren't carrying anything superfluous, like real pilgrims.

*11.00*

In Belgorod they decide to take a look at the town first, after all it's interesting to see how people live here, then to take what they came for and return by the evening suburban train, there's plenty of time, there's no need to rush, so they exit the vomit-strewn railway station of the formerly glorious Rus' town and immediately they come upon a store with an enormous quantity of alcohol inside. Nah, what's the point of dicking around in Belgorod, says Vasia, and enters. No one contradicts him.

"What would you boys like?" asks the saleswoman in Russian. "Mamasha, mamasha," says Vasia the Communist, "a little vodka." "How much?" asks the saleswoman.

"Two," says Vasia. "Twin-packs?" she asks in a businesslike manner. "Crates," says Vasia. "Boys, are you sixteen already?" Together they all pull out their student cards with the state symbols of their republic. After that the drawbridge is lowered and they are sold the vodka.

"It would have been good to screw her," says Sailor back at the station. "Young man," Vasia replies irritatedly, "are you here for business or fucking?" Basically a rhetorical question.

*14.00*

On the road back they got beaten up by the border guards. Basically it was their own fault, they let themselves go knowing they had the goods in hand, let their guard down and smoked up right in the carriage, and since the carriage was almost empty the border guards practically had no choice, they just walked up to the boys and laid into their backs with batons. The boy scouts remained silent and so as not to express their pain and despair they thought about something good, and because it—this good—was right next to them, under the benches, the thinking was easy and they endured the punishment with dignity. The border guards were obviously expecting some armed resistance, they had been yo-yo-ing back and forth on the train for several hours, you have to see it from their point-of-view, you spend your time traveling on this stinking suburban train along the nation's border and there isn't even anyone to start a fight with—it's all just speculator-housewives, nobody you would want to start a brawl with, they beat up the boy scouts simply out of inertia, just like that, to stay in shape, though it didn't make anyone feel any better.

"Assholes," says Vasia, when the border guards disappear. "They should go work in the factory, on the shop floor." "Right," says Sailor, "in the foundry." Everyone agrees—right, in the foundry, the foundry, the foundry—that's a good one.

*18.00*

At the railway station in Kharkiv they find some hutsuls who have spent the last two months making their way from somewhere near Kostroma, where they'd been working, and have now been sitting in the Kharkiv station for several days, they have spent all their money and don't know where to go—back to Kostroma to earn some more money, or just head home because the season is over; they decide to head home, they pool the rest of their money and buy one of the crates of vodka from the boy scouts, the vodka that the scouts are selling is cheaper than anywhere else at the station, so the hutsuls take the crate immediately, who knows what will happen later, better not to take a risk with this kind of thing.

Vasia and his pals suddenly find themselves with a pile of money. The two nameless guys immediately demand that it be divided, but Vasia tells them—fuck no, we'll do as we agreed, the youths insist; Sailor clearly doesn't know how to behave in this situation, no one has ever in the course of his life divided money in his presence, so the youths decide that he's also on Vasia's side and they don't dare to simply smash their faces, okay, they say, then just remove our vodka, fuck you—Vasia sticks to some kind of communist principles and refuses to share, then the guys take a bottle in each hand from the bag, which is how many in total—four bottles—and take off, you can give us back the camera later, they say in parting and disappear into the dark underpass. "What's with them?" asks Sailor, he doesn't like the situation, it was such a nice group, they drank vodka, talked about life, no one offended him—Sailor—and then suddenly this. "You see," says Vasia the Communist, "how money spoils people." "Not me," says Sailor. "You don't have any," answers Vasia the Communist and goes off to sell more vodka.

But sales seem to have stalled, the platforms are empty, everyone who wanted to travel has obviously already left. Vasia can't think of anything better to do than go back to the hutsuls, and the hutsuls are so drunk already that they agree to take the vodka, okay, they say, and take several more bottles from Vasia, after which Vasia also expertly foists a bottle onto some granny who is waiting for something hopelessly with her grandson fidgeting by her side, he's about seven-years-old, in fact it's the grandson who advises granny to take the bottle, take it, he says, it will come in handy on the road, granny scolds him but listens to his advice and takes the bottle, so Vasia is left with very little to sell.

From the neighboring platform they have been observed for some time now by three serious dudes in adidas track suits, they approach Vasia and Sailor, force them into a circle and say, who are you?

Vasia begins to explain. The guys listen, then this obviously bores them and they say, listen, we asked, you know, just for decency, but really we don't care who you are and where you're from, and how many of you there are here, this is what we want to tell you: if we see you here again we'll bury you over there, somewhere between the first and second platforms, and then every evening the Kyiv express will blare its horn over your graves, but for the time being we're not going to do that (after this the terrified Vasia relaxes a little, but the terrified Sailor does not), in general, we sell all the liquor here, you might say this is our territory, and you're certainly not needed here (Vasia and Sailor suddenly realize this is true) and now that we've had a little chat with you here, we can see that you are not really competitors, you simply appear to be retards (both mentally agree with this), so we're not going to do anything to you this first time, but as compensation ("Oh no," thinks Sailor. Vasia maintains a terrified silence) we're going to take your vodka. Not all of it, you see what honourable outlaws we are, remember that. They look in the bag and take a bottle each, oh, and one more thing—we wouldn't have paid any attention to you, but you're selling vodka too cheaply, you're undermining the price, get it, retards?

Vasia and Sailor run into the underground passage and catch their breath. "Assholes," Vasia takes up his old tune. "They should be sent to work on the shop floor." But Sailor no longer finds this funny, let's go home, he begins, fuck, says Vasia, there are five bottles left, we'll sell them and then leave, they'll kill us, says Sailor, cut it out, says Vasia, what are you afraid of, we'll do everything quickly, buy some grub and set off home, come on, don't be afraid, no, says Sailor, I don't want to, I'm afraid. Okay—Vasia loses his temper—to hell with you. Here's some for your work, shove off: he pulls out two bottles and gives them to Sailor. Sailor hesitates for just a second—all things considered, he thinks, in the morning I had nothing. Now I have two bottles. Obviously that's a plus, he decides, and takes the honestly earned vodka. Okay, take off, says Vasia, we'll see each other at home. "Yes, he really is a retard," he thinks, watching his companion leave, his tired, thick-set army-navy figure disappearing into the dark passage. It is also getting dark on the street, the first stars appear, and the birds hide from the rain in the railway building. "If I go home now," thinks Sailor, "I can lock myself in the shower and drink everything by morning." And that is what he does.

*21.00*

He takes everything that he's got left and walks along the evening platform, you have to take risks, whether you want to or not; when you're 19 and your head is full of naked women from the front pages of newpapers, advertisements, and propaganda, why should you be afraid on the third platform of Kharkiv's South Station. At 21.00 the non-stop train for Baku makes a stop, the conductors are from Baku, reliably flush with cash, they're worth a try. Vasia approaches the first carriage, they tell him to clear off, he goes to the next one, then in the third a thick-set Baku commissar stops him, "The vodka's not poisoned, is it?" he asks, "It's good vodka, good," says Vasia, "Okay, hand it over, let's go in the wagon," "Why in the wagon?"—Vasia suddenly turns very tense, "don't be afraid," says the commissar, "I'll just check whether it's real vodka or not, if everything is okay. I'll take the whole lot at once." They enter the conductor's compartment, where it smells of hashish and expensive tobacco, the carriage is warm and half-empty, almost no one is going to Baku, and those who are are sleeping, it's nine in the evening, what else is there for them to do, they're afraid of going out onto the platform where they might get caught up in yet another customs search, they'll buy vodka from the conductor later, it's better not to show your face in the station, they all smell of sperm and hashish from several yards away, as though the whole journey, for several days and nights, these citizens of shithole Azerbaijan have been jerking off after smoking up, "come in," says the conductor to Vasia, Vasia steps inside the dim compartment and the conductor slams the door shut after him, "sit there for a while," he says, locks the door and goes off somewhere, Vasia starts to panic, kicks the wall with the toe of his shoe, knocks at the closed door, circles like a rat in the tiny room that reeks of Asian grasses, finally sits on the numbered blanket that covers the shelf and begins to cry as he's squeezing a plastic bag with the vodka under his arm. Well, okay, he says to himself, okay, don't whimper, what can they do to you, well, they can take away the vodka, to hell with the vodka, think—it's only vodka. They can fuck you. Yes, they could fuck you, especially that boar in the railwayman's beret that shut me up here. No, they wouldn't fuck me, how could they fuck me, but Vasia looks at the table strewn with cigarettes and condoms, and thinks that basically they could fuck him. They could sell him to the Chechens for the spare parts they need. Do the Chechens need me? Of course they do.

For organs, they'll cut out my kidneys, lungs, balls, tie me up somewhere by my feet in one of their auls and they'll start pecking at my liver as if I were Prometheus, or they'll flay me like a rabbit and they'll make a Chechen war drum out of my skin, my mother won't even come from Cherkasy to visit my grave, I've got to get out of here, get out before the guy from Baku returns; Vasia takes off his belt and ties the handle on the door with it, now they won't get in if they try, he tries to open the window, it gives a little, Vasia sticks his head out into the fragrant railway dusk, he presses down some more, the gap widens, Vasia catches his breath, sees several porno magazines on the shelves and pushes himself with determination into the window. Here the train jerks harshly, its rheumatic joints screech and it sets off in the direction of Baku, dragging—along with everything else—the innocent Vasia the Communist, who's my friend, by the way.

It's always like that: whether you like it or not you have to struggle, otherwise nothing will come of anything, you can either sit at home and keep still or make an effort, grab the tough circumstances by the balls, and afterwards, if everything works out, then the jack-pot will certainly be waiting for you, whatever it is that winners get in such cases—a discount card, permanent sale prices, free sex—in a word, you better hustle cause otherwise you'll never get out of this shit; Vasia looks with despair as the last railway building sails past him, the speculators and smugglers disappear, even the cops are no longer visible, in this situation he would have been pleased to see them, but the entire collection of endearing and familiar objects is disappearing somewhere into the blue yonder, and just then the commissar from Baku finishes his simple dealings, remembers the hostage, and tries to enter his own compartment. But the door won't open. Hey, infidel, open up, he shouts something along these lines. The carriage waits in alarm. Vasia moves about feverishly in the window and suddenly realizes that he's stuck. The conductor has no idea what's going on. He speaks in his customary Azerbaidzhani generously interspersed with words from the brotherly Slavic languages, at first he simply curses, then he becomes alarmed—what if the boy scout is having an apoplectic fit? Then he nervously begins urging Vasia to heed his conscience and to observe public order, he calls on the passengers to be witnesses, the train is by now somewhere in the suburbs and here the window frame in which Vasia the Communist has gotten stuck is unable to withstand the load and cracks, Vasia has just enough time to collect himself, turns himself around in the window and quite expertly, like a courtyard cat used to being dragged around, slips out the window, the wind bursts into the conductor's empty compartment and joyfully throws into the air all the cards, condom wrappers, and pornographic postcards, ruining, to put things succinctly, the established daily routine of this loyal servant of the Ministry of Transport of the Republic of Azerbaijan. The endless train full of bags of coal and suitcases of heroin happily wags its tail and soon its leading carriages enter the territory of Russia, in a word, you cannot envy those guys.

*23.00-08.00*

Vasia doesn't even break anything, we're not talking about the carriage here but about himself. He simply rolls down the embankment and tears his right pant leg, but he doesn't even drop or break the vodka—which he was convulsively pressing to his heart all this time—not to mention all kinds of ribs, tibia, and other anatomical shit. He gets up as though nothing has happened, shakes off his pant leg, wipes his sweating palms on his sweater—careful so that the vodka doesn't slip out of his hands—and goes off in search of civilization, but what kind of civilization do you expect when you have just fallen out of a railway carriage—you have to walk wherever you can, along factory fences, past what was once the pride of the defense industry, and only the earth splats beneath your feet—sticky and tenacious, like a piece of chewing gum. But suddenly Vasia finds himself on the rails of a streetcar line, well, this is okay, he thinks, all I need to know is in which direction, he sits on the rails and brings out his bottle. He takes a few swigs and considers hiding the bottle, but then decides not to hurry, why hurry, he thinks, I'll make it through to the morning, and then things will become clear, and he continues to drink and doesn't worry too much about this night and all its unsuccessful business. Everything is fine in principle, everything is fine, things could have been much worse, they could have killed me or strung me up somewhere in the carriage vestibule, or fried me in a furnace, those Tungus bums, Vasia puts his lips to the bottle with relish, yeah, he thinks, it's a good thing that there's a lot of vodka, I won't even be able to finish it all. It's a good thing too that I won't be able to finish it, because where could you buy any around here now. Although if the need arose I could make a trip to the railway station and buy some from the hutsuls, he thinks, and sits there, in his torn jeans that are falling down without a belt, in a dark sweater and worn sneakers, on the wet rails which reflect, from time to time, the piercing rays of moonlight.

At one in the morning Vasia is almost run over by the next streetcar. Only at the last moment does the driver notice that there's something on the rails, a dog, he thinks, and decides to crush it, but he still has time to notice that no, it's not a dog, not a dog at all, dogs don't down vodka from a bottle, he just has time to brake, runs out of the streetcar and finds the drunken Vasia on the rails. What are you—a moron? he shouts, I almost cut you in two, you fucking idiot! Sorry, says Vasia, I got separated from my train, here have some vodka, the conductor takes the bottle, a little is good for stress, he says to himself, and sits down besides Vasia. And so they sit there on the rails, without even talking, they just sit in silence and don't get in each other's way—the rails are wide, there's enough room for everyone, a light rain begins to fall, okay, says the driver at last, let's go, I can give you a lift to the park, you can make your way back from there somehow, thanks, says Vasia, but you have to buy a ticket, there are controllers on the line, what controllers? Vasia says in amazement—it's nighttime; oh, says the offended driver, you're used to traveling without a ticket, fine, it's time to go, and they climb into the cold streetcar and drive to the park, on the way a woman controller really does get on, walks up to Vasia, who wants to pay her, searches in his pocket, but finds only a thick wad of Russian rubles there that he bartered from the hutsuls, and that's all, nothing else, here, he says to her, take this. What is this? she asks, money, says Vasia, dirty money. Take it, please. But the controller suddenly says: not a chance, I don't need that kind of money, give me ours. Where can I get it from? Vasia fights back exhausted. From wherever you like, says the controller ruthlessly. I got separated from my train, says Vasia, but the controller doesn't react. Well, if you like I can give you some vodka. No, refuses the controller, I don't want any. Really? says Vasia in astonishment.

"What can you say in a situation like this," he thinks. "You cannot get a ticket, or pay the fine, a total bummer in short." He gets out of the streetcar, sits on the rails and takes out a second bottle. The wet shining rails stretch smoothly away from him, out in both directions into eternity, and it is precisely this that to a large extent reconciles him to reality.

## INTRODUCTION NO. 4

*22.00*

When I become an adult and am 64, I will recall all this tedium, if only to establish whether I myself have been transformed into a slow-moving animal that employs its nickel jaws merely to chew grub stored for the long polar winter. What will I feel like at 64? Will all these children of the streets and supermarkets hate me too, the way I hate everyone over 40 who has succeeded in digging themselves in on the green hills of this life, precisely on the sunny side? And what will I think of them? What do you have to do to your brain over the course of a life to prevent it from finally rotting and becoming a pile of slimy seaweed useless even for making food? I suspect that even if I discover something about this it will be when I'm 64 and won't want to change anything. What's happening to all of them? They also obviously began as decent cheerful inhabitants of our towns and villages, they obviously liked this life, they couldn't at first have been the depressing jerks that they have become now at the age of 50 to 60. If so, where are the roots of their personal great depression, what are its causes? Obviously, the cause is sex, or Soviet rule—personally I can't think of another explanation. I like to look at old photo albums, with photos of the '40s and '50s, in which these cheerful young guys with short haircuts always smile at the camera dressed in military or technical school uniforms, with simple and universally necessary things in their hands: monkey wrenches, depth charges, or at the very least model airplanes—these children of a great people, flag-bearers, holy smokes, where did all this disappear, the USSR squeezed everything human out of them, transformed them into a processed food ready for

Uncle Sam, that's what I think. In any case I constantly notice the hatred and aversion with which they observe their own children, they hunt them, catching them in the silent corridors of our enormous country and lay into their kidneys with the heavy combat boots of social adaptation. That's how it is.

*19.00*

With so many doors in front of you, you never know which you should enter, I think, standing in front of the streetcar. This is the third or fourth that I've let pass, I just can't concentrate and decide what I need and why. Which is to say where I have to go and who is waiting for me there. I have somehow unexpectedly been left alone, without friends or acquaintances, without teachers or guides, only passengers stand here next to me on the last stop, in the rain, they push themselves into the streetcar and, it seems, I'm in their way. In any case they look at me in an unfriendly manner, that's for sure. And then, when I more or less figure out what I want, two figures in raincoats and epaulettes emerge from behind my back and take me with them, at first I resolve to jump into an empty streetcar, but this one is going, well, nowhere near my destination and it wasn't my day—they grabbed me by the arms and pulled me across the square.

*19.30*

It looks like an army barracks. And it stinks like an army barracks, come to think of it what does it in fact stink of? canned meat and deserters, idiotic cannon fodder, that's what it stinks of. In a glass booth sits a guard with a sawed-off kalashnikov, he's reading porn and stuffing his face with canned food, picking it from the tins with a folding spoon. When we entered he didn't even move, that's what you call military training and iron nerves. In the corridor several large lamps hang from the ceiling, in fact the light is not very bright, but my tears have been flowing for about the last half hour, I can hardly see anything, so the lamps blind me, I cannot even make out what kind of canned food the guard is eating. He lets us through without a word, and they don't even greet one another, an ugly people these sergeants, ugly and strict, like Finns or Laplanders. They just hate me, I noticed this at once while still there, at the last stop, those raincoats of theirs, no, they definitely hate me, the fascist scum, they sit here eating their canned food, I would be at home now if it wasn't for these Laplanders. Externally they appear to be ordinary guys, maybe a few years older than me, in different circumstances we could become friends, go to soccer games, the cinema, I don't know, whatever else friends do, yes but people can deteriorate very badly, all they need is to put on the trousers of some uniform, I can only imagine what will happen to them in the future, it won't simply end here, they themselves should understand that, these Laplanders.

*19.15*

Okay lad, says one of them, obviously the senior guy, or the most fanatical. Either you walk ahead or we kill you now. Wait–wait, I say, you don't understand, I'm clean, let me walk, but in the other direction, in the direction I was going. Where you were going? shouts the senior, you got stuck in the door, people couldn't get in. Seriously? I ask. Well, someone pushed me forward. Who pushed you? he shouts. You simply threw yourself under the wheels and then got stuck in the door. Okay-okay, I say, let me go back there and try again, okay? And I really do try to free myself from their embrace, and it's then that they start beating me. And when this doesn't help they take out the gas tanks and generously douse me all over, while turning away themselves. Obviously they dislike the smell.

*22.30*

And you, you bastard, who only yesterday did completely insane things on account of your innate alcoholism and cheerful nature, you suddenly find yourself prepared to support all forms of repression and all punitive operations, to waste your time at home reading the crime news and to support not the honest and mad maniacs but the generals from staff headquarters and the brutes from special forces, you become an old reactionary jerk who has forgotten the aroma of the regional offices of Internal Affairs. That's how fascism begins—yesterday's fighters on the invisible front suddenly become transformed into a rich support base for inhumane experiments with reality and consciousness, those who only yesterday returned from the front and its trenches as victors, now, after some ten or fifteen years, find themselves suddenly transformed into fascist pigs, this is the greatest secret of civilization, society devours itself, it becomes heavy and sinks under the weight of the silicone with which it has pumped itself up.

*19.45*

"So," says one of the fascists, "take out whatever you have in your pockets."

"I can't," I say. "First take off the handcuffs."

"Don't fuck around."

"Well, at least take them off temporarily, I'll take out my stuff, and then you can put them on again."

"Well, yes, we'll take them off and then you'll try to run away again. Come on, pull your stuff out, or you'll get hit on the head again."

"You have no right to beat me," I tell the fascists. "I'll phone the dean."

"We're the ones who will phone the dean," say the fascists.

"No, he's my dean, so I'll phone him."

"You talk too fucking much," they say.

Yes, our conversation just isn't clicking. I wonder where their gas chamber is, I still cannot see very well. On top of that, the gas combined with what I've already drunk is making some kind of rainbow concoctions in my head.

"Now we're going to photograph you."

"What for?" I ask.

"As a souvenir," laugh the fascists.

"And where's your gas chamber?" I ask.

"What?" they fail to understand.

"You know, the chamber," I say. "With the gas."

"Oh, you mean the shower," they say. "Coming up."

Now they're going to shoot me, I think, the fascist scum. And here a stout captain enters the room, not in the meaning of a ship's captain, he's about fifty, with some residue of good conscience in his eyes and some residue of sandwiches on his uniform jacket. I grasp immediately that this is my chance and decide to hang onto him—well, not by the uniform of his jacket, of course.

*23.00*

After that comes old age, you're simply empty inside, there's just nothing left in you, it has all been squeezed out, you've been wrung dry and thrown out, so now you can take pride in your artificial limbs and medals. Who needed you, what did you do for the most part all this time, why does everyone hate you and why can't you answer them in kind? Where is your own hatred? Where is your fury? What has happened to you? What has the system done to you? How did it all happen—you began pretty well, when you still were 16 or 17, you were a decent person, not completely polished and with a future not yet wholly predictable, how come you got into this mess, how will you look the angels in the eyes at the security checkpoint after dying in your own shit, how will you look them in the eyes, what will you tell them, they won't understand you, they don't understand anyone, no one at all.

*20.00*

"What do you want to be?"

"A teacher."

"What kind of a teacher can you be? You're a total drunk."

Yes, I have to start getting out of here, because this scum is going to shoot me for sure. It appears I made a mistake. You can never trust these fascists, they will always betray you.

"May I ask, sir, what's your name?"

"Mine? Hm. Mykola Ivanovych. Mykola Ivanovych Ploskikh."

"What?"

"Ploskikh."

"May I just call you Mykola Ivanovych?"

"Go ahead."

"Mykola Ivanovych…"

"Well?"

"You know, I don't drink at all."

"I can see that."

"Seriously. I don't drink. At all."

"Then how come you got so plastered?"

"Mykola Ivanovych, you see… It was my dean."

"What dean?"

"Well, it was his birthday today, you understand?"

"Ah, and so the whole faculty was boozing?"

"Well, no, of course. He just asked for help in moving. To a new laboratory."

"What laboratory?"

"A new one. To move. To transfer things there, the equipment—"

"Equipment?"

"Well, yes. Retorts."

"What retorts?"

"You know, retorts—those, kind of—" I try to explain to him what a retort looks like but I can't remember.

"So?"

"We're chemists."

"I can see that."

"Seriously. You know, they have various retorts." (Why am I stuck on those retorts?) "Mykola Ivanovych…"

"Well?"

"Do you have children?"

"Yes," says Mykola Ivanovych, straightening the jacket of his fascist uniform. "A son. The same kind of fuck-head as you," Mykola Ivanovych appears to let himself go a bit. "He's started to sniff glue, the parasite. I got into his nightstand the other day."

"Got into his nightstand?" I fail to understand.

"Well, I had *my* things in there, you understand? I got into it and looked; there's no glue, so I say to him—so, you little prick, first you smoked *my* cigarettes and now you're sniffing *my* glue?"

"Your glue?" I don't understand him at all. What is he talking about?

"I bought it to do some home renovations" says Mykola Ivanovych, offended. "For renovations, is that clear? And how can I do any renovations now, without glue?"

"Right," I say.

"And why did you throw up over yourself?"

"I don't know, Mykola Ivanovych, I have this problem with my nose recently. I sleep badly, can't catch my breath. And I throw up."

"It's your glands."

"You think so?"

"Sure, it's your glands. You should have them cut out."

"Cut out?"

"Uh-huh."

"Well, come on," I say. "How can I cut them out? What will I have left then? Maybe my glands are the best thing that I have."

"Oh sonny-boy, sonny-boy. What am I going to do with you?"

"Mykola Ivanovych—"

"What?"

"Let me out. I won't do it any more."

"How can I let you out? In your state they'll pick you up again in five minutes. Those same two assholes who dragged you in will pick you up. They're young, for them it's just like shooting down an enemy airplane—you get to paint another star on the fuselage. So, just sit here. At the moment you're safest here. Okay, now, where are *my* keys—let's go. I'll leave you in the cell until morning.

"The gas cell?"

*20.30*

It's dark in the cell, along the wall there are two benches, on one lies a young guy in a leather jacket, between the benches is a window with a steel grating over it, Mykola Ivanovych collects my belt and shoelaces and leaves me in the dark. I immediately rush to the window, it can't be, I think, that nobody can escape from here, one can escape from any gas chamber, obviously one can escape from this one too. What are you doing? asks the young guy, his leather jacket creaking in the dark, I'm trying to get out of here somehow, oh, right, says the guy, then dig a tunnel. You don't mean, I say, that there's no way out of here? None, he says, none. A tunnel is the only way. How do you know? I ask. I sat in this same cell, he says, three and a half years ago, when they picked me up the first time. Wow, I say, so you're at home here? Follow the conversation, man, says the guy, how can I be at home in the cop shop? Sorry, I say, I didn't mean to offend you. What did they pick you up for? In the slammer, says the young guy instructively, his leather jacket creaking offendedly, they don't ask what for, in the slammer they ask what're you charged with, understand? I understand, I say.

We sat together like this until morning. He talked about the slammer and I thought about my own stuff. The benches stank of bedbugs.

*18.06.93 (Friday)*

*7.00*

"Mykola Ivanovych?"

"Okay, sonny-boy, get up. We're going for rehabilitation."

"Goodbye," I say to the young guy, but he just creaks sleepily in reply.

So here's how it is: Mykola Ivanovych leads me down battered corridors, out through a side door, I see that we're in the corridor of the passport office, which is also in the same building as the district police station, there is absolutely no one here yet, no visitors, only two cleaning ladies who are washing the corridor from both ends and who give me reproachful looks, each in her own way of course, but reproachful. Mykola Ivanovych opens another door and leads me into a large room with an old fridge and a gas stove, the floor is covered in whitewash, it looks as though they are repairing the room, maybe this is the gas chamber, I think, and they obviously poison people using the gas stove.

"Right, sonny," says Mykola Ivanovych in a business-like manner, "right."

Now, I think, he'll propose that I put my head in the oven and he'll turn on the tap.

"I have decided not to telephone your dean. What do you need that unpleasantness for, right?"

"Right."

"But I don't want this to happen again, is that clear?"

"Clear."

"Well, then," says Mykola Ivanovych, "here's your passport, and here's your belt."

"And my shoelaces?"

"Oh shit, I forgot them. Well, I have to go back anyway. Okay, here's the thing," he doesn't seem to know himself what he wants. "You see that bulb?"

"Yes."

"It's broken, see?"

I look up. It really is broken.

"I see," I say.

"Well, unscrew it. Because I can't climb up there. MY years won't let me."

"Unscrew it?" I ask to make sure.

"Unscrew it."

"And that's all?"

"That's all."

"And then I can go home?"

"Well, no," says Mykola Ivanovych. "You'll stay until evening, so nobody can say anything, and then you'll piss off, to wherever you want."

"Until evening?"

"Until evening," says Mykola Ivanovych. "Go on, climb up."

He positions the wobbly folding ladder for me—it's covered in whitewash and paint— and steps aside. He's probably afraid that I might fall on him. I shift about and hesitate but decide to climb; whatever you say, this Mykola Ivanovych is not such a shit, he is a shit of course, but not that bad, at least he gave me back my passport, even though he did lose my shoelaces somewhere. I climb up and examine the bulb up close, it's not just broken, it's some kind of a poor excuse for a light bulb, all covered in whitewash and paint, I don't know who takes care of repairs around here but whoever it is obviously has a hatred of electricity.

"Well, how is it?" asks Mykola Ivanovych from below.

"In good order," I say.

"What good order?" shouts Mykola Ivanovych. "You little jerk, unscrew it. I don't have time to play around with you."

And here somewhere in the depths of the building, on the other side of the wall, a gunshot is heard, then another, then a round from a kalashnikov, a real firefight, I almost fall off my ladder, well, I think, okay, Mykola Ivanovych thinks the same, obviously he's scared, he pulls out his makarov and disappears into the depths of the passport office. And I'm left on the folding ladder. The shots die off. What's going on? I think. I try to unscrew the bulb some more and suddenly get an electric shock, again I almost fall to the floor, fuck your district police station, I say, with its passport office included, I climb down the ladder and walk out of the room. On the left is the freshly washed corridor, on the right is some door. I turn the handle. The door opens. Outside, in the courtyard of the passport office, by the door, stands a white volga and that's it, no one else, no visitors, no passport inspectors, no towers with machine-guns and barbed wire. I walk out and stand by the door. Basically, I think, they could shoot without warning. Behind the door another shot echoes. I walk to the gate, open it and go home.

*8.30*

At the last stop of the No. 38 streetcar stands Vasia the Communist, he is standing by the kiosks and holding up his jeans. Greetings, I say, what's with you? Oh, says Vasia, I got separated from the train. Where are your shoelaces? Ah, I say, I lost them. I see, says Vasia, shall we have a drink? Okay, I say, except that I don't have any cash. Mykola Ivanovych took it all. What Mykola Ivanovyvh? asks Vasia. Ploskikh, I say. What? Ploskikh. I see, says Vasia, well, let's go, I have some. What's that smell on you? he asks again. It's not cognac, is it? Bedbugs, I say. What begbugs? It's a long story, I say. I see, says Vasia.

How's your business? I ask when we have bought some. Ah, says Vasia, not good. I decided to quit. How come? I ask. Well, you know how it is, says Vasia, it's impossible to do an honest business in this country. On top of that the dollar exchange rate keeps jumping around  I see, I say.

*8.47*

At home we find our friend Dogg Pavlov. Greetings, says Dogg, as though that was what was expected—what's up with you—have you brought some booze? We have, says Vasia, we have. What exactly? he sniffs  it's not cognac, is it? Cock-nac, I tell him, and where were you?

At the soccer game, says Dogg, we spent all last night there, but no joy at all. So we're all staying inside—we haven't seen each other for a while, and there's plenty to talk about after all.

"Dogg," I ask. "How'd they play, by the way?"

"Who?" Dogg fails to understand.

*Part One*

## WHOSE DEATH DO YOU WANT FIRST

*9.15*

This lyrical story begins with a guy in a blue coat carrying a plastic case who appears on the doorstep and spends a long time turning a piece of paper in his hands, looking to see if it's the right address, whether he has come to the correct place, whether someone has bamboozled him, in short—a gloomy, dispirited guy, with this case, on top of it all. Generally speaking I don't know where such people come from and where they are written off afterwards. Finally he plucks up his courage, knocks at the door, enters, and sees us all—me, Vasia the Communist and our friend Dogg—we smell of morning booze and evening barf, in a word—a workday morning. The guy starts turning the paper in his hands again. Who are you?—asks Dogg. Of the three of us he is the most scared, because after hearing the sounds of a funereal dirge yesterday, that is to say after he slipped like a fish out of the inexperienced hands of Vova and Volodia, it's on his own close-cropped head that he expects to feel the next installment of bad luck, so he's thinking, I wonder if they're coming for me, someone from the editorial office, maybe a hit man, who knows who those assholes have on staff, it's a wealthy newspaper, they could easily rent an assassin by the hour from among former intellectuals, someone who, for instance, used to work recently as an engineer in an institute and now after the default, with unemployment and the disintegration of a big country, has become a free-lance hit man—Dogg is terrified, he's convinced, and in the room silence reigns.

"My name is Robert. Uncle Robert," says the guy, at last putting away his piece of paper. "Where's Sasha?"

"Sasha who?" I ask. Maybe I missed something and some girl called Sasha has moved in with us. In that case the hit man is after us all.

"You know, Sasha, he's supposedly living with you. This is ..." he says, again takes out his piece of paper and begins turning it around nervously.

He? Sasha? I think. Is she some sort of hermaphrodite, this Sasha?

"You know—Sasha," Uncle Robert says pleadingly. "He left this address at home, said that he lived here. And told us about you, well, described you, I even imagined you like this," he says and smiles in a friendly way.

Like this? I think. How does he mean? Covered in barf?

"Ah," Dogg is the first to catch on. "He's talking about Carburetor, about Sasha."

"Ah, yes, of course," everyone relaxes at once, it turns out there never was a girl called Sasha among us, and that's a good thing. And this screwy Uncle Robert, it appears, isn't a hit man, although it's hard to say anything nice about him either. He continues to smile at us in a friendly way. Dogg also begins to show some interest in him, not exactly in him but more in his plastic case; obviously, thinks Dogg, if this screwy Uncle Robert has come to see Carburetor—this is how he thinks—then maybe he's brought him something tasty and nourishing, he hasn't brought crankshafts at any rate, more likely, after all, something tasty and nourishing, there must be, thinks Dogg, some eau-de-cologne in there or marijuana, eau-de-cologne would be better in the morning, I hope it's not crankshafts, in short, at the moment we're all having trouble understanding who this is and what he's talking about. He continues:

"So, you are—Sasha's friends?"

"We," says Dogg without taking his tipsy eyes off the case, "are friends."

"And what's this," asks Uncle Robert, trying to gain our confidence, "drinking cognac in the morning?"

For some reason I immediately stopped liking him after that—some sycophant with a case, standing there talking bullshit.

"Yes, they are." Dogg points at us. "Come on in, sit down. Would you like some tea?"

Dogg last drank tea about two years ago, when still in school. And now just look at how chatty he has become.

"And where's Sasha?" asks the guy worriedly.

And here everyone starts to think—where's Sasha? somehow in the last few days everyone had forgotten about him, I had for sure, it turns out that everyone had business of his own, his own problems, well, you know how it is—you run around doing your stuff and then it turns out you don't even know where your friends have disappeared.

"Maybe he's in class," I say doubtfully.

"No, I've been there," says Uncle Robert. "They told me that classes ended more than a week ago."

"Really?" I ask.

"Yes. They suggested that I come here, to your place."

"Well, that's right," says Vasia to calm him somehow. "That's right. Where else should one look for him?"

"Dogg," I ask, "was he at the soccer game with you?"

"No,"says Dogg. "Although in principle," he addresses Uncle Robert directly, "I lost consciousness there, so I don't recall very well, maybe he was."

"So what has happened?" I ask.

"Sasha has a problem," says Uncle Robert, and sits on his case by the entrance. I think to myself that it is actually empty and he carries it around with him to serve as a chair.

"What problem?" I ask.

"His father."

"But he doesn't have a father," I say. "He has a stepfather."

"He was like a father to him," says Uncle Robert.

"Wait a minute," says Dogg suddenly, "a father and a stepfather are completely different things. Although," he adds, "in principle they're both just dicks."

"Wait," I tell Dogg. "Why do you say—was?"

"He died," says Uncle Robert. "The day before yesterday."

"How did he die?"

"Shot himself."

"How?"

"He had a rifle."

Carburetor told us about the rifle. Generally he didn't like to talk about his parents, but he told us a few things here and there, it all sounded screwed up, his father left them when he was still very young, then this guy with the rifle turned up. Carburetor used to say that he was a deadbeat, that he was constantly boozed up, that he would go and shoot every living thing in the neighborhood, he would be taken away time to time but would then be set free together with his rifle, it sounded like something from the Wild West if you listened to Carburetor. He also told us that his stepfather had only one leg, not because he was born that way, of course he wasn't some sort of pathological monster, they simply amputated it at one point, this was during the USSR, but the stepfather had been in his own civil war, from which he returned on an artificial limb. Carburetor loved to tell this story, he relished the details, playing all the roles—in a word, the story appealed to him. As I said, the stepfather dragged a rifle around with him everywhere, a nice collector's item, if Carburetor was to be believed, there was a whole group of crazy scalp hunters there, half of them without licenses, but one of them worked in the regional prosecutor's office so they could even have raced around in panzers if they wanted, no traffic cop would ever have stopped them, they hunted all year round without paying any attention to the season, they would just get boozed up, take a cop car and race off into the steppe in the direction of the Russian border as far as their gas tank would take them, and, as I said, in so far as the USSR was still holding itself together and here was no border, they would just race until they ran out of gas and then, having petered out somewhere in the middle of the spring or winter crops, they would make their way back home however they could, carrying each other, instead of trophies, on their shoulders. I liked this story too, I didn't understand Carburetor in principle, your stepfather, I would tell him, is such a comical screwball, what do you have against him, you should go on a trip with him and come back with some mammoth hide, I could imagine such a trip, basically they could have raced like that all the way to the Caspian Sea, like redskins in the prairies, shooting all the fauna around them, and then when they reached the Caspian they could have shot a whole pile of camels or whatever lives there by the Caspian, and then they could have returned, very cool; but Carburetor didn't like that kind of stuff, or maybe he liked it but didn't let on. In any case, on one occasion during one of their regular booze-ups, the drunken company drove off into the countryside and got stuck again, so they had to spend the night there. In the morning the combines came upon them, because it was harvest time, not hunting season, and they had gotten stuck somewhere right in the middle of a field that was being harvested. The combines were driving at a distance of a couple of hundred meters from one another and suddenly these redskins appear in front of them, or more accurately—red-faced guys with rifles. At least that's how I imagine it. The nearest combine, which was driving directly at them, began to swerve away and at this moment its reaper got stuck, so the combine stopped, the guy climbed out and quietly cursing the hunters began to stick his leg right into the jaws of his Satanic contraption, trying in this way to clear the clot that was jamming the blades. Carburetor later showed us a diagram, it looked frightening, on the diagram at least. No safety procedures were followed, of course. Who's going to turn off the combine for something like this! After all, it's a question of the struggle for the harvest and all that crap. And here the hunters who still felt that they were on the hunt, suddenly decided to help the guy with the combine, I don't know why, maybe their conscience spoke up, though that's hardly likely, probably they simply found it fun to deal with a monster like this Nyva agricultural combine. "Nyva!" "Nyva!" Carburetor shouted—in this whole story what appealed to him most was obviously these giant machines—and then this stupefied stepfather also stuck his leg in and even cleared the jammed blades, and the cutter's metallic teeth began to turn, swallowing into its jaws the next portion of the people's harvest, along with the stepfather's right leg. They had time to pull the guy back, but without his leg. Things could have been much worse, though. As it was, his leg was bitten off up to his balls, at least that's what Carburetor said. I tried to imagine what happened after that—okay, I thought, he was already missing a leg, they probably drove him to the hospital, although how did they get out of there? On combines or what? Well, okay. And what about the leg? The big agricultural inside of the combine, as I imagine it, was already packed with several hundred kilograms of golden grain, mixed with the stepfather's cartileges and veins as well as inorganic matter—you know, an army boot, a pant-leg—in short, a pile of raw material; it would be interesting to know what the grain farmers did with all this stuff, they certainly didn't dump out a hundred bushels of grain, they probably delivered it to the state, I'm sure they did, I know these despicable grain farmers, they'd deliver their own shit if someone accepted it, and then I go on to imagine the baking and the bread, in a word—a simple boy's bloody fantasies, you know how it is. Anyway, the guy lived on, now with only one leg, but, as I understand it, this was quite sufficient for him, at least he continued to booze and shoot everything that moved, like some sort of monster.

"How can you shoot yourself from a rifle?" Dogg raises his voice. "It has a long barrel, you can't aim it at yourself."

"Well, what about the ricochet?" asks Vasia.

"Oh, sure," I say, "you think he first fired and then threw himself at the bullet, right?"

"No," says Uncle Robert. "He pressed the trigger with his foot."

"He was missing a leg, right?" I ask.

"Yes, his right one," says Uncle. "He pressed with his left."

"What, was he left-handed?" asks Dogg.

"Dogg," we all call him to decency.

"Can you imagine?" says Uncle Robert. "They found him and at first couldn't even recognize him—half his head had been blown off. They recognized him by his sock."

"So you must have a lot of one-legged hunters out there?" I ask, but Uncle Robert doesn't even get offended.

"So where is he now?" asks Vasia.

"In the morgue. The funeral is the day after tomorrow."

"The day after tomorrow?"

"Yes, in the afternoon. They'll try to assemble the pieces of scull, you see."

"What if they can't?" I say.

"Don't know, they'll cremate him, probably. We have to find Sasha, so that he can attend. I've been at his lecture hall but they said to look here."

"He's not here," says Vasia.

"Then where can he be?" asks Uncle Robert.

"Well, stay here," I say, "and wait a bit."

"I can't. They're expecting me at home. My sister needs help with the funeral, then I need to go to the morgue, they'll try to put his head together, it has to look like him."

"Are there a lot of different possibilities, or what?" asks Vasia.

"Listen boys," Uncle Robert gets up off his case and approaches me, "find him. My sister wants very much for him to be there. They didn't get on well, but he's gone, understand? That's the way it is. And you still have time, until the day after tomorrow. Find him. I brought you this." He opens the case and takes out three bottles of cognac.

"You don't have to," I say.

"Yes, really, you don't have to," says Dogg and takes the cognac.

"Find him," says Uncle Robert and goes into the corridor, his figure bent over, and doesn't say goodbye. I don't know, maybe he loved the deceased, who can figure out these redskins.

"Uncle Robert," I say, "Uncle Robert. What a strange name—Robert. Sounds like the title of a gay magazine."

*11.15*

"Well, what do you say?"

"I don't know. It's scary."

"What is?"

"Well, this Uncle Robert. He's some kind of hit man."

"I think he's a asshole."

"You think so?"

"He's an asshole for sure. Did you see his case?"

"Yeah ..."

"What are we going to do?"

"Don't know."

"Maybe we should look for Carburetor?"

"How will we find him? He's not attending classes. I don't even know where else he goes."

"Does he have any friends besides us?"

"I don't have a clue."

"Yeah ..."

"Then there's this Uncle. An asshole."

"That's for sure."

"Carburetor will be upset."

"You think so?"

"Sure he'll be upset. It's his father, after all."

"Stepfather."

"One and the same dick."

"Carburetor didn't like him."

"Still, it's family. These kinds of things, they really touch you."

"No they don't," I say. "Naturally, I have nothing against it—family, parents, it's all okay, I'm okay with this stuff. It's just that it really isn't as important as it seems, it's just that everyone has this tendency to say 'family, family' but in reality they don't give a damn, they get together only at funerals and memorial services, and that's all. Do you understand?"

"Well, no," says Vasia. "I disagree. I love my parents."

"When did you last see them?"

"What's the difference?" says Vasia. "I don't need to see them to love them."

"Listen," Dogg suddenly says to him, "can you imagine yourself at your parents' funeral?"

"What's with you? Are you off your rocker?" Vasia is offended. "What are you trying to say?"

"Nothing in particular," says Dogg. "Me, for example, I probably wouldn't get invited to the funeral, that is, if they ever converted."

"And how do you imagine that?" I ask. "Do you expect a special telegram: 'Dear Dogg Pavlov, please come, there are now two Jews fewer in this world!'?"

"Well, I'm not talking about that."

"What then?"

"I don't know, I just think that if something happened to them, they would blame it on me, they've gotten used to blaming me for everything."

"You're just an anti-Semite," I say.

"All the same," says Vasia, "you're disclaiming family ties. In their own way they're fun."

"What, memorial services, you mean?" I say.

"No—you know, parents, family. As soon as I finish up here I'm gonna pack up and go home. My mom's in Cherkasy."

"You know," I tell him, "I've got nothing against it. A family's a family, a mom's a mom. You know, my brother and I once, when we were still in school, cleaned out a palace of culture, a small one. We walked off with the equipment."

"Why?"

"I don't know, we just had this strong desire to do it, we decided we needed to clean some place out. We dragged out some amplifiers, various sound mixers, even part of a drum set, can you imagine."

"And so, what did you do with it?"

"Sold it. To another palace of culture. They didn't even ask us where we got it, the suckers. Basically we sold it for cheap, so there was no incentive to ask. We sold it. And then we went to a store and bought some disks."

"Disks?"

"Yes. A pile of vinyl, and on top of it the guy, the one selling it all had under the counter a genuine Depeche Mode, think of it, they had just put out their live double album. *10*, it was called. Well, we put down a pile of money for it."

"Really?"

"Yes. And you know what was the best part?"

"What?"

"This was just about the only thing that my brother and I bought TOGETHER."

*11.35*

Shit, what should we do, I don't think we should go looking for him. Why does he need this, and the deceased—why does he need it, he didn't even need him very much when he was alive, and now he's on the road to his Valhalla, limping through the cosmic darkness on his single leg with nothing but angels standing along the path, giving him a military salute, with fingers raised to their foreheads, or raising arms torn off in battle—the deceased is obviously going to a heaven for invalids, there must be some discrimination there, they don't let them all go through the same gates—though, how should I know? Really, how should I know, maybe it's precisely the thin and long-legged angels in SS helmets, who hold their Schmeisser submachine guns in front of them and assemble the healthy and the invalids in front of enormous illuminated gates with a sign written in a script designed by Rodchenko that says "Work Makes You Free." They bring everyone together, whoever tries to escape is simply shot down and dragged to the neighboring clouds, finally Saint Peter comes out, a kind of Buratino with a huge golden key, he opens the gates and the angels begin to drive the masses in, pushing them, and there; inside the courtyard of this lousy heaven they divide them into columns and lead them along various roads, each of which, nonetheless, inevitably ends at an enormous gas chamber.

Therefore the guy still has two full days left to make it to his final stop and come to a standstill forever in his depot, after surrendering his weapons to the angels and obtaining a large iron cross from them for heroism on the eastern front. The fact that he voluntarily dropped his brains onto the kitchen floor doesn't count for anything—there are moments in life when it is the most honorable and greatest of moral acts to release the people around you from your presence, and you have to make allowance for these things.

Actually, there is one district that's kind of an old factory suburb—it lies just past the new circus, stretching from the river right up to the railway station, square kilometers of an impassable private property, immediately behind which the factories begin, a kind of suburb to the factories, you might say—during the summer you won't meet anyone on the streets there, I have no idea where they all go, but you can clamber about for hours over the sand and gravel without meeting a soul, I won't even mention what it looks like in the winter. Here's what I'm getting at: our friend Chapai lives there, in a workshop at a plant that makes equipment for miners, not hammers and picks, but various lights, lanterns and so on—everything that's useful for a miner at work, Chapai says that his grandfather built this plant, so it's kind of a family tradition with them, Chapai's father took to the bottle a few years ago and spent time in a lunatic asylum getting cured, Chapai would visit him occasionally, bringing fresh underwear and newspapers, greetings from brigade leaders, that kind of thing; they lived in one of the barracks right on the river, but then these barracks were leveled, and since in the eighties Chapai the elder had already drunk away all the documents, including the pawn tickets for the St. George Cross and the Order of the Red Flag that the grandfather had received, naturally no one was going to find them a new place. Chapai junior, as the regimental son, went to the director of what was then still a normal Soviet factory and asked to work on the shop floor, in his father's trade, as it were, part of the dynasty and so on, Chapai was good at that kind of thing; I even think that by then he had already reserved a place for himself in the lunatic asylum, in the same ward as his father, that would have made it a kind of ward for exemplary workers—teams of pioneers could have visited them on trips, listened to their depressing and maniacal stories, and left them packages filled with oranges, cookies and denatured alcohol on the bedside tables. Representatives of strong professions have to die beautifully, only various intellectual low-life is allowed to drown in slop and suffer from hemorrhoids, but real men who firmly grasp in their right hands whatever-it-is that they grasp in their right hands—who grasp in their right hands the levers of life's chief mechanisms—they have to die at work, fall heroically on the hot foundry floor, suddenly bringing to an end their workplace seniority, dying from delirium tremens and overdrinking, from the various traumas of daily existence, if delirium tremens can be considered a trauma of daily existence.

So where am I going with all this? The director agreed to take him on at work, they fixed something in his documents, and because Chapai had not finished school yet and had no intention of doing so, the director simply brought him into the factory. They allowed him to live in one of the workshops, in the storeroom in fact, with the greasy overalls, and told him not to worry about anything. The director was also in a way part of the dynasty, if you can imagine a dynasty of red directors, although—why not. The plant had by that time begun to lose ground in the market for manufactured miners' accessories, or whatever they are called, well, that's to say there was no market as such, they were considered the only high-profile enterprise in the republic, the factory was starting to fall apart, like everything in the country, whatever could be stolen had been stolen by the director, everything else had been broken by him, in short he acted according to the old civil defense instructions and, foreseeing the advance of the treacherous though invisible enemy, had blown up the machines, the water pump, and the communication just in case, not in the literal meaning of the word, naturally some things continued to work—several workshops, and the company cars kept rolling along somehow—but the general enthusiasm had disappeared and the workers had crawled off into the private sector. Nonetheless, Chapai and the director remained. Later the director had a change of heart and decided to revive at least a part of his exclusive progeny, evidently the ghosts of dead red directors would visit him at night and wave their miner's lamps in front of him preventing him from sleeping, so he started up the business again, found some investors, they reentered the market with some new product and although most of the plant's territory remained mired in crap and ruin, the general impression was that the plant was operating. I'm saying all this because Chapai continued to live in his workshop, expanding his domain to two little rooms, he now worked as an auto mechanic, though he partied at every opportunity, despite which the director liked him, as a specialist, that is. And Chapai, since he had so much free time, took up with the local punks and got some real distilling equipment, which he constructed from diagrams using pieces of some special equipment he had collected in the factories and workshops, even attached a certificate of quality to it, the entire diabolical machine shone with nickel, copper and secret aviation duralumin; the director had nothing against it, let him occupy himself, he said, if his soul loves technology—he didn't quite understand, I think, what Chapai was running through the retorts, but the shine of the nickel serpentine tubing calmed him, the more so since Chapai paid for the electricity himself, and the main thing is one's ability to count up every penny earned by workers; as for trade unions, marginal profitability, government support, he never understood any of that junk. And so—here's what I'm talking about—through the punks who would buy from Chapai their hundred grams of alcohol—the commissar's gift for a job well done—Sasha Carburetor got to know him, Sasha was not a punk, in fact he didn't like punks, he liked technology, as I think I've already said, it turned out for some reason—someone introduced someone, someone had a female cousin, someone slept with someone and got two ribs broken for doing it—anyway, it turned out that they became acquainted, Sasha and Chapai, and Sasha would sometimes go to Chapai's workshop, look at the shining and sweating serpentine tubing that was doing the distilling, he would pore over the equipment's diagrams with Chapai, drink the still unsettled mash from a liter-sized mug, well, in a word, all this was his world—not just the mash, but the whole thing, the equipment, the serpentine tubing, the heavy and machine-building industries—Carburetor needed this, and Chapai had a whole plant full of this crap including the surrounding district. So, if our Carburetor was to be found, it was probably there—in the plant's workshop, that's what I'm thinking and I lay all this out in front of my friends, yes, really, there aren't that many places that would let our kind in, and Carburetor had such a place for sure, and so we slowly get ready and start to leave and then unexpectedly, outside, we come across Cocoa, Cocoa is standing in front of the entrance to the stairwell, looking sort of soft and swollen, he sees us, oh—he says—greetings, where are you off to? we, says Vasia, have some business, so go to bed. Can I come with you? asks Cocoa, wiping his sweat off with the sleeve of his jacket, the fat nerd; go on, off to bed, says Vasia sharply; I don't want to go to bed, Cocoa continues to plead—take me with you; fuck off, Vasia loses his temper, you're all we need. Well, where are you going, at least? asks Cocoa plaintively; Cocoa, Vasia says to him, we have business, can't you see? we're looking for Carburetor; Carburetor? really? then listen—says Cocoa; forget it, snaps Vasia, go to bed; look, friends, I can help ... says Cocoa in confusion; , goodnight, and off we go off, leaving him behind, the pudgy fool.

*12.00*

Humid foliage sticking to you, wet papers, red buildings—somehow our trip was not a great success; we managed to cross half the city, we made it into the square, as though we expected to find our friend on the street, finally we get pushed out of the trolleybus by the ticket inspectors, and now we continue on foot, cross the square, walk on, looking at the posters, looking at the advertisements, there's nothing else to look at, Dogg is dragging a backpack with booze; near the bake shop there's a crowd of crazy hippies, they've crawled together like rats seeking fresh air, they stand around drinking something, and near them are some familiar faces, Sasha Chernetsky is there, and someone else in a leather jacket with badges and medals; we know Sasha, Dogg and I even went to his concert a couple of weeks ago in the palace of culture that's by the stadium, the bouncers drove us out—someone next to us threw a firecracker into the hall, they thought we did it, we barely got away; the crazy hippies are standing by Sasha, it's a nice morning of a nice day.

"All non-conformists should be shot," says Vasia.

"Trotsky said so?" I ask.

"What does Trotsky have to do with it? Look at them standing there, the sons-of-bitches."

"So what?"

"I don't like it," says Vasia and walks on in silence.

In half an hour we cross the bridge, find the plant's fence, and crawl through a hole into the yard.

*12.30*

We had visited Chapai several times before, he chose his workshop with his friends in mind, because there were several other ones around—half-ruined gray buildings dating back to the first Russian revolution of 1905. Chapai's workshop has "socialism" written on it in green paint and a somewhat rickety star resembling a jelly fish—in color, that is—that was painted on later. Chapai, like Vasia, knows dialectics, they respect one another, it's me and Dogg that are foreigners here—I simply don't like Marx, that's all, but Dogg has his own issues with the old man, you don't have to ask why.

Chapai recognizes us at once; greetings, he says, enter, he lets us into the store room, pokes his head outside, looks around guardedly and shuts the door behind himself. We enter. Chapai, as is the custom among proletarians, cultivates a certain life-style, his room is almost empty, in the middle stands the apparatus I have already mentioned, humming alarmingly, under the apparatus there are various retorts, I finally recall what they look like, on the windowsill lie books, I take one—the fifteenth volume of something, I can't quite make out of what, but clearly of something to do with the party, it bears the stamp of the plant's library, he's a serious lad this Chapai, he's older than us by a couple of years, he's already over twenty, and on top of that he has working experience—he's not just anybody, he follows us into the room and asks us to sit down; in the room there are several low stools; how are things? he asks; okay, says Vasia, we're here looking for Carburetor, have you seen him recently? Not for a long time, says Chapai; he sits on a stool, throws one leg over the other and lights up a Bilomor.

Chapai is thin and intense, he pays almost no attention to us, sits by himself, leg over leg, reading some party propaganda, he's wearing an old T-shirt, sneakers and track pants, and he also has glasses, among our friends there aren't many who wear glasses, though maybe he does this just for show, I don't know.

"You wouldn't know where he might be?" I ask.

"No, I don't."

"He didn't say anything to you?"

"Nothing."

"Bummer," I say. "His father died."

"Stepfather," Dogg corrects me.

Chapai remains silent.

"He didn't by chance forget his stuff here?" I continue.

"No."

We can talk this way forever, he speaks in some sort of mantras, having read Engels, and doesn't process normal information, these new communists have their own mixed-up Zen, which you can't really get into, and if you do, you can't get out of it, you'll be spinning your wheels on the slippery tracks of Marxism-Leninism without understanding a thing.

"You reading something?" Vasia asks him suddenly.

"Oh," answers Chapai. "A couple of books were dropped off here. I'm looking through them."

"Uh-huh," says Vasia, they are like-minded thinkers, we try not to get in their way.

"Is it okay if we wait for him here?"

"That's okay."

"We have some booze."

"So do I," Chapai points to his apparatus. "Only I don't drink."

"Why's that?"

"The clap."

"Really?" I place the book back on the windowsill. "Where did you pick that up?"

"Right here, at the plant," Chapai replies calmly.

"At the plant?"

"Yeah."

"There are only guys here."

"Right."

"Who did it to you?" I ask. "Sorry, I mean who did you do?"

"Who—did what?" Chapai fails to understand.

"Well," I say, "do you know who you got it from?"

"Ah," says Chapai, "from no one. I have lifestyle clap."

"What do you mean, lifestyle?"

"Just that. Lifestyle. I don't have sex at all. We were loading some second-hand stuff, and that's how I picked it up."

"I see," say I. "You Marxists are simply angels—you don't fornicate, you don't drink."

"You load second-hand stuff," adds Dogg.

"Listen," says Chapai, obviously so as to change the subject, "do you have any dough?"

"Why?" says Vasia cautiously.

"We can go visit the Roma, get some dope. Then we'll sit here and wait for your Carburetor. Otherwise just sitting here is no fun, I don't drink, you see."

"Okay," says Vasia, "we can go. Do you think he'll turn up?"

"Who knows," says Chapai. "Maybe he will, maybe he won't. By the way, you don't need any rags, do you? There are some jeans and sneakers over there. Second-hand, of course ..."

*14.00*

Vasia agrees to shell out for the taxi, he seems to have finally given up on the idea of going into the vodka business, obviously he's not that kind of guy, he is unable to make money on something sacred, so we follow Chapai out—Chapai, Vasia and I; Dogg we leave by the equipment, sort of to keep the fire going, so that he can keep an eye on things and place a new retort under the serpent from time to time, Chapai showed him how but gave him strict orders not to drink from the retort, saying it was not hygienic; you rotten clap-carrier, Dogg says to him, why don't you shut up; they start getting worked up but we pull them apart; more precisely, we drag Chapai out into the street, where he relaxes—because he really does have the clap, there's no denying it. As a rule there are no taxis in this part of town, there are excavators, but even they are rare, so we hoof it as far as the circus, by the circus it's deserted, grass is growing through the gray slabs, it looks like it's going to be a nice summer; if we could also get Carburetor to the funeral, things would be great; Chapai tries to catch a car, the drivers are alarmed by his blue track pants and no one stops, in the end he succeeds in stopping something and we cram inside and drive to the Roma, avoiding rainbow-colored puddles.

*14.40*

The Roma live in a different end of town, past a different river, they have an entire settlement there, the Kharkiv Roma have in their own way realized the ancient Roma dream of a sacred Roma megapolis, they didn't have to get into great conflicts and all the rest of it—battles for independence, struggles for territory, demarcating boundaries—they just settled en masse, but in a compact manner, by the river, dug themselves in as best they could and in effect dissolved into this hostile eastern capital, in this way they got a kind of illusory City of the Sun, a city within a city you might say; there were streetcar lines that ran through their district and there was even a branch of the subway nearby, but in reality, apart from the Roma there was almost no one else living here, so if you found yourself here (though, why would you ever find yourself here) and didn't know where you were, you would simply be amazed by the number of Roma on the streets, that is, not that they were actually that many of them on the streets, but simply that they were the only ones on the streets, so you would immediately notice there was something odd without being able to figure out what it was. The Roma lived a collective life and had dug in for a long stay—they had built strong, low buildings out of white brick and surrounded them with walls made out of the same brick, which made their places look like brickyards, it was hard to even figure out what goes on in there, behind these white brick hills, quite amazing to look at. The Roma didn't have antennae or radio transmitters, there were almost no advertisements either, it was some kind of medieval district, I think the walls were so high to prevent the plague from getting into their yards; I could never understand these Roma, but it was here that Chapai had a dealer friend, on a quiet side-street, first you have to drive the dusty district for a long time, then turn off the main street to the right and stop there. The driver lets us out, spends a long time turning the Russian money over in his hands, calculates the exchange rate, how much we owe him, turns down the fingers of his right hand while counting—I, for one, cannot count like that—then says, good, that's enough, we get out and he quickly takes off.

*15.10*

So here we are standing among the small hills of white brick, there are almost no trees, the earth is soft beneath our feet, a toxic grass is fighting its way up from under the walls, above, behind the clouds the sun appears from time to time, and there's not a single Roma in sight. What did you expect, I think to myself, these people live without antennae, without transmitters, without Soviet rule, even without numbers on their houses, now the interesting part is how Chapai is going to find his dealer. But Chapai is good at orienting himself in such situations, he adjusts his glasses, sniffs something out, and then says—it's here, I've found it. We approach some rusting gates and Chapai begins to hammer with his fists on the rusty pockmarked surface, while taking the opportunity to inform us that his dealer—Yurik—is in his own way a cool dude, he was born somewhere around here, but, to be sure, he wasn't a successful Roma, after school he tried to make his career in the party and the Roma damned him, smashed his face and drove him from the district, although he would have taken off himself because they had given him a nice apartment in the center, he worked, I think, in the Kyiv regional committee, in the cultural department, though what kind of culture could there be in the Kyiv regional committee? For a Roma he did pretty well and they were already getting ready to promote him to the oblast committee, but here his genes took over and—according to Chapai—he either stole something, or screwed someone, in short, he messed up, got kicked out of the regional committee, but remained in the party, they didn't have that many Roma in the party, they sent him off to do similar party work as the head of the club at Chapai's plant, he played the accordion there and organized the chess games. When the plant began to fall apart, Yurik hung on at the club to the very end, by that time he was boozing shamelessly, he would come to the club in the morning, take his accordion and play something from Kobzon, to every melody adding something of his own, something Roma. According to Chapai, Yurik degenerated morally and physically, pissed in his pants right on the club's stage, slept in his own vomit, wrapped in some agitational banners, and this went on until the plant's director took away his accordion and sold it in the marketplace, putting the proceeds, a rather miserly sum according to Chapai, toward the plant's external debt. Yurik pulled himself together a bit, his apartment had already been taken from him by some shareholders' bank, which gave him some shares under the table as compensation, Yurik tried to sell them off somewhere but naturally no one would take them, in a word, his life had come full circle and Yurik had no other choice but to return to his medieval district with its white bricks and strict hierarchy. However strange it may seem, Yurik was welcomed as a native son, the Roma are a communicative people, they smashed his face one more time and forgave him everything, at the same time they took his illegally obtained shares and succeeded in selling them somewhere, sticking them on some sucker farmers, although they didn't share the money with Yurik, but that was their own affair, they knew best. Yurik settled down peacefully in one of the brick buildings behind a white brick wall, he didn't hang around the center anymore, even wanted to get married but couldn't find a wife—obviously their medieval customs forbade them from marrying a communist, it's a good thing they didn't burn him at the stake; he gradually got involved in their community life, at first he sold chewing gum in a kiosk, then took things to a higher level and started selling vodka in a store, then—higher still—sold dope, and finally he just stayed at home, selling the life-healing herb to whoever needed it, whoever didn't need it was told to piss off and he took shots at them with his Berdan rifle from behind the brick wall, having pulled up the drawbridge and flooded the moat with water. He remembered Chapai from his time working in the club. Chapai was a steady client, though it was clear that there was something Chapai wasn't telling, at least that's how it seemed to me.

*15.15*

After a few minutes the bolt on the door screeches and the dealer's head appears. Yurik doesn't look like a Roma, in any case I imagined the typical Roma differently, naturally I didn't expect some guy wearing a red shirt with large polkadots and carrying a stage-prop guitar in his hands, but we did learn something about the Roma in school, and here this thin albino comes out in a worn gray suit and with a cataract on his left eye and looks us over suspiciously; he and Chapai begin whispering something, taking a close look, practically sniff one another, finally the dealer gives us a sign with his hand and we follow him. I'm curious what lies behind the battlements—cannons, battle-axes, torture equipment—but everything is peaceful, there's a little shed made of white brick standing in the yard, by the house there's a dog kennel, also made of white brick, there are some chickens lying in the kennel, one of them has climbed onto the kennel and is standing there, oh, chickens, I think—actually, that's all I think—and we enter the house. In the room stands a table and nothing else. The walls are bare, on one, it's true, hangs an expensive kilim, whose edges have been hammered in with nails, you can see the nails easily, they are okay—good, solid nails. Yurik says we should wait here and, flashing his cataract, goes into the neighboring room, Chapai is nervous for some reason, although he pretends for our sake that everything is okay, in a moment we'll get some, I examine the nails in the kilim and suddenly see a large fish on the windowsill, I don't even know what kind of fish, I could never distinguish them—fish, you know, frogs and all that—the little window is open and there are several bees flying around the fish, circling lazily, who knows where they came from after the recent weather, they were sleepy and completely unaggressive, although maybe that's how they are supposed to be. They land on the fish's flesh, crawl along it, I walk up closer, try to turn the deceased thing over and immediately pull my hand back—inside the fish has been completely devoured by these winged carnivores, there's an entire hive of them in there, when I touch the fish, they all fly out and circle around the fat body, but they soon settle down and fly inside once more, how disgusting, I think, a dead fish, a dead gypsy fish, devoured from the inside, what a horror.

Yurik enters with a package of dope, sees me by the fish, and can't tear his eyes from it either, the bees crawl in again, and there's something so horrific in this that we all gaze transfixed at this devilish fish—me, and Vasia, and Chapai, and Yurik—and even the crucified Jesus visible under the latter's shirt looks very attentively at the Roma fish that has been devoured by bees and cannot turn away. Yurik finally puts his package down on the table, and we start to sniff it, feel it, look at it in the light, in short we give every impression that we know what good dope looks like and that you cannot screw us, even if you are three times a Roma and the former director of a club, we can see right through you and we can see right through your dope, although in reality we cannot see a thing, Vasia takes out a wad of notes, counts them off, Yurik watches piercingly with his cataract, Jesus looks on very attentively, Yurik complains that he will have problems with the rubles, he has to deal with the exchange rate and it's not clear where the dollar stands right now; the dollar is doing fine, says Vasia, the buck is standing firm, your prick is standing firm, Yurik says to him, but he takes the money and leads us out onto the street, I still hear how the bees quietly move their feet in the fish's belly, though, perhaps, it only seemed to me that I did.

On the street Yurik parts from us coldly, we walk off about ten meters, Yurik continues to stand at the gates without entering the yard, and at this point Chapai finally lets his feelings show, he suddenly stops, hang on, he says, we can have some fun with him, what's with you, I say, what for? he's there all alone anyway, didn't you see, he won't do anything, forget it, Vasia says frightened, let's get out of here, everything's okay, it's okay, says Chapai, don't piss your pants, I'm just going to get him worked up, he takes the package of dope, pokes around in it as though he's checking it, puts it back into his pocket, turns around and goes toward Yurik, a few meters from him he stops and shouts:

"Your dope is shit!"

Oh, fuck, I think, fuck.

"Shit!" repeats Chapai with more assurance.

And here Yurik suddenly takes off and disappears in the yard, we don't know what to do, that is, Vasia the Communist and I don't, but not Chapai—he, it seems, knows what's coming, clearly this is not the first time he has had some fun with his dealer, so he quickly returns and shouts at us to run fast, and we really do run fast and, it has to be said, not without cause, because the gates behind us open again and Yurik jumps out of there with his Berdan rifle, and sparks are flying from his eyes, even the one with the cataract is giving off sparks, although not as strongly, we run, our main goal is to reach the corner, where civilization begins, with its streetcars, subway, fairly normal relations between people, by contrast behind our backs there is Yurik with his Berdan and his medieval castle and its chickens and killer bees, there's plenty to run from and we're starting to tire, Vasia has it the worst—his belt is missing, he holds his jeans up with his hands so as not to lose them, meanwhile Yurik pulls the trigger and fires into the sky above our heads, once, then a second time, he doesn't even aim at us, thank God, otherwise who knows how things might end, he fires into the sky and laughs gleefully, I hear this quite clearly as we turn the white brick corner, the fresh summer wind hits us in the face, lifting into the air the trash, dust and feathers, and these feathers twist above our heads, so I can't even tell what they're coming from—whether from birds in a brick palace or, perhaps, from angels who have just been shot, who have flown to Yurik to lighten his medieval loneliness, while he, the fool, has driven that snow-white amiable flock away into the rainy sky and has been left alone, standing there in the middle of the empty Roma megapolis—a solitary-lonely dealer, seller of joy, duped by fate, who doesn't even have anyone to talk to, only Jesus swinging sadly on the cross—from left to right, from right to left, from left to right.

*17.00-20.00*

"You're just unable to understand it. You just say Marxism-Leninism but don't understand what it is."

"Well, yeah, you're the only one here who understands everything."

"What have I got to do with it. It's not about me. You're talking about Marxism. In reality Marxism is winning, understand?"

"Well, of course. And where is it winning, then?"

"Marxism isn't winning in any one place. It's winning in principle."

"Oh, sure."

"The power of Marxism lies in its self-sufficiency. Take Trotsky."

"Trotsky was a Jew."

"Yes. Do you know why Trotsky traveled to Mexico?"

"In my opinion, Koba gave him the boot."

"Koba was a Jew too."

"Koba?"

"Yes. And Illich too."

"Illich was a Kazakh."

"A Tatar."

"A Kazakh."

"What's the difference?"

"Kazakhs are illiterate."

"And what about the Tatars?"

"They are too."

"No, Koba wasn't a Jew. Koba was Russian. His surname was Russian—Stalin."

"That wasn't his surname."

"Whose was it then?"

"It was his son's surname. Vasia Stalin. He was a soccer player."

"Oh, right, and Trotsky was a basketball player. In the labor reserves."

"What does Trotsky have to do with it?" Chapai repeats the phrase that I'm already used to, sitting on his stool and lighting a joint. "Trotsky has nothing to do with anything. You," he says to Vasia, passing the joint to him, "ought to understand that. They," he exhales in our direction, "will never understand this, they are infected with the bacteria of capitalism, but you," he takes the joint from Vasia, takes another drag, and returns the joint to Vasia, "should understand it. You know about the theory of permanent fuck-all-ism?"

"What?" Vasia starts to cough and passes the joint to me. "What fuck-all-ism?"

"Permanent," Chapai adjusts his glasses. "Well, that's my name for it. Generally it's known as the theory of the permanent collapse of capitalism. But I prefer to call it the theory of permanent fuck-all-ism."

"Yeah," interjects Dogg, taking the joint from me, "permanent fuck-all-ism—that's cool."

"What's the theory?" I ask, awaiting my turn again.

"The theory is simple," says Chapai, letting out the smoke and passing the joint further down the circle. "It was developed by comrades from the Donetsk oblast committee."

"Oh," I say, "they are capable of that."

Chapai looks at me questioningly.

"Countrymen," I explain.

He nods his head in agreement, pulls a three-liter jug with some kind of fruit juice from under the table, takes a swig, and offers it to me. No, no, I wave my hand in refusal—I prefer to smoke.

"So," continues Chapai, using his sleeve to wipe the bloody tomato-colored liquid from his mouth. "The theory is in its essence revisionist. It is based on a review of Marx's main ideas. Ideas related to the self-sufficiency of the proletariat as such. Have your read," he turns to me because Vasia has disappeared somewhere behind the smoke, "the correspondence of Marx and Engels?"

"No," I say, "but I know they were friends."

"Correct," says Vasia, "they were friends. And good friends, don't doubt it."

"Clearly," I say, "good friends."

"And their correspondence was cool," says Chapai, "in its own way even cooler than *Das Kapital*."

"What could be cooler than *Kapital*?" inserts Dogg, a little off subject, but I pass him the joint and he shuts up.

"In the USSR," says Chapai, "*Das Kapital* was recognized as the fundamental work. This, in my opinion, was the main, tragic mistake of Soviet ideology. It should have paid attention to the correspondence. To the correspondence of Marx and Engels. The comrades from the Donetsk oblast committee have proved this," he says confidently and finishes the roach.

For about twenty or thirty minutes everyone remains silent, thinking about the comrades from the Donetsk oblast committee. Finally Chapai gets his mind back and begins rolling another joint.

"In one of the letters," says Chapai, taking a drag and passing it to the unconscious Vasia, "this is from the early correspondence," he explains, "from the so-called Hamburg period …"

"Like The Beatles!" I say.

"Marx at the time was experimenting a lot with social consciousness."

"What?" These words wake Vasia up.

"Chapai is saying," I explain, "that in his day your beloved Marx, in Hamburg, on the Reeperbahn, experimented with expanded consciousness."

"He took acid," Dogg can hardly wait for his turn and shows obvious signs of agitation.

"And as a result of these experiments," continues Chapai, "the EWC principle was revealed to him."

"The what?"

"External Workers' Cell," says Chapai. "The idea is simple—first they show you a false picture of production relations. The falseness," says Chapai, "lies above all in the supposed permanent growth of capital. That's a fiction," says Chapai decisively, grabbing the joint from me out of turn and taking a deep drag.

"What's a fiction?" I say, failing to understand and trying to take the joint back from him.

"It's all a fiction," says Chapai after thinking a moment. "The proletariat is self-sufficient. Therefore the only ideal and ideologically sound principle is that of external working cells, the so-called EWC. The external working cell on its own is also self-sufficient."

"Listen," I say, "your Marx is some kind of Buddha—"

"Not to speak of Engels," inserts Vasia from sleep.

"This is how it works. Each EWC is formed according to the anthill principle. The basis of the formation is each separate enterprise, whether a plant, a factory, or some other entity. And around this entity the EWC gathers like ants around an anthill."

"Yeah?" I ask. "And who plays the role of the queen ant?"

"The party committee," says Vasia confidently.

"Oh," I say, "so everybody gets to fuck the party committee."

"The party committee," Chapai repeats confidently.

"Fine," I agree. "So, what else?"

"That's it," says Chapai. "Social life is constructed according to this principle, if Marx is to be believed."

"And power?" I enquire.

"Power is not necessary. In this system power is redundant. Power—that's a fiction too. You, for example," Chapai turns to Dogg ahd tries to get the joint from him, "do you need power?"

"No," says Dogg, "I don't need it."

"And you?" Chapai turns to me, while keeping one eye on the joint.

"Well, some kind of primary, minimal kind," I say.

"That's it," Chapai says solemnly and grabs the joint from Dogg. "That's it. Primary. That's exactly what I'm talking about. Only primary power is absolutely necessary, power built on the principle of autonomy. Everything else is fiction. Every other, more structured power doesn't function. And, therefore, is unnecessary," and he passes me the joint like some audience appreciation award that I have just won. We all forget about Vasia, as he does about us.

"Generally speaking," Chapai continues, "most structures and institutions are unnecessary, so all this crap has to be minimized and gradually destroyed."

"And what does your Marx tell Engels should replace this?" I ask.

"The PuC principle," says Chapai.

"The what?" even Dogg enquires.

"Proletarian Charter," says Chapai.

"Proletarian Charter, that's PC, and not PuC," I say.

"Yes, I know," says Chapai. "That's just for euphony. The PuC principle sets all this in motion, the charter plays the role of the elementary unificatory mechanism. Any further accumulation of capital is brought to an end and its progressive disintegration begins."

"How's that?"

"All very simple." Chapai again puts his mouth to the blood-red jar. "In principle, following the earlier unnecessary and poorly motivated accumulation of capital, an excessive concentration of the means of vital activity has occurred, and as a result the only logical outcome in this situation is the collapse of existing resources."

"How's that?"

"Well," Chapai tries to explain to us, "to keep it short—in reality nothing needs producing. Each separate EWC can survive independently for several decades by means of existing resources. This significantly simplifies the mechanism by which society functions. In practice it looks approximately as follows—let's take our plant, for example. An EWC is created around it, which in turn is subordinated to the local PuC, each EWC takes over a certain number of local objects in the general infrastructure, takes power and runs everything into the ground."

"What for?" I don't understand.

"Here lies the essence of the principle of permanent fuck-all-ism," says Chapai. "We destroy the structure and feed off the obtained raw materials. For instance, we gain control of a bank, but spend the money on the survival and the functioning of the EWC, we gain control of the shopping centers and distribute all the rags evenly among the members of the EWC, we gain control of the offices and take all the working equipment for ourselves, we gain control of the taxis and put them to work for the cell."

"You gain control of the farms and give everyone a cow," Dogg suddenly inserts.

"Yes," says Chapai, "that's it. In short, the comrades of the Donets oblast committee have provided the economic foundation for all this, they have calculated everything, conducted serious monitoring surveys." Chapai pulls out some notebooks and waves them in the air: "It turns out that the existing social infrastructure, the whole contemporary base of capitalism, is capable of feeding itself for at least another 67 years."

"And after that?"

"What do you mean, after that?" says Chapai in confusion. "Afterwards they'll think of something. In principle the theory is new, it hasn't been tested in practice, some changes will, of course, need introducing. But in general," he repeats, "one shouldn't get hung up on the further growth of productive forces—on the contrary, production should be cut back as much as possible, conserved, in a word, and natural resources saved as much as possible since what exists is already enough to last the next 67 years."

"That's cool," I say. "I really like the bit about shopping centers. And about the farms," I tell Dogg.

"Yes," agrees Chapai, "the idea is quite correct. The main thing is that it's fair, without any added capitalist clap-trap."

"Wait," I say, "but how is your PuC going to control all this—after all, there's a whole pile of things that need to be centralized."

"For example?" asks Chapai.

"Well, I don't know. Transport, for example. The subway."

"What's the subway got to do with it?"

"Well, not the subway," I retreat. "But, let's say, airlines. How will your PuC control them?"

"There won't be any airline companies."

"What do you mean there won't be any?" I say in surprise. "So how will people fly?"

"What do they need to fly for? What REAL benefit is there from it? You, for example," he focuses on Dogg, "have you ever flown in an airplane?"

"No," says Dogg, "I basically use streetcars."

"See," says Chapai, "and it's the same for most of the population. Airlines, airports, stewardesses—it's all a fiction. In reality there is no REAL need for it, understand? We need to leave only what is REALLY necessary."

"Okay," I say, "and what about the army?"

"There is no REAL need for the army. What benefit is there from the army? The army was created only to justify the necessity of its existence in our eyes. To this end wars are organized from time to time, bombardments, revolutions, the defense complex operates, scientific-technical potential is built up, a system of propaganda is created. But there is no REAL need for this—if the army was dissolved, society would still continue to function normally, you see, therefore there just isn't any NEED for it."

"Okay," I say again, "what about the security organs?"

"What?" Chapai takes a drink from his blood-colored jar.

"You know, the internal organs. The militia, police, the KGB, CIA, and all that. What are they—a fiction too?"

"Yes, they are a fiction."

"The KGB is a fiction?"

"A fiction."

"Really?"

"Absolutely."

"I like that," I say.

"Look, have you ever had dealings with the KGB?" Chapai continues his persecution of Dogg.

"Yes," Dogg says unexpectedly, "they came to our school once—I was already in the tenth grade, and a KGB guy came. He talked about the work, did his agitation. Said something about the president."

"And so?"

"Nothing. I was impressed, basically. I went up to him in the corridor afterwards, said, 'Commander, can I get a job with your outfit?' He told me to get lost. He says, 'Your breath smells too bad for you to work in the KGB.' And that was it."

"See," Chapai says to him instructively. "All the power organs work EXCLUSIVELY for the support of their own existence—they produce nothing, there is no NEED for them. If they were to be closed tomorrow, nothing would change. Nothing would change if the borders were opened or closed, if the diplomats were let go—one can simply live without external politics. And without internal politics too, in principle. One can live without administrative personnel, with the disappearance of administrative personnel all the other problems for whose solution they have been created also disappear. One doesn't need offices, housing controls, governments, administrations—so one doesn't need any documentation, and vice versa. The EWC controls all that minimal production process that guarantees society's vitality for a whole 67 years. Everything else comes from the devil," says Chapai triumphantly, and he passes me a new joint, but I'm sinking deeper and deeper, like my friend Vasia, pushing aside the heavy blue water with my arms and legs, and I see before me only the worn soles of his old sneakers, so I swim after them and from there I hear:

Life is a spaceship, and once you have climbed into it you have to sit still and not touch anything, just be ready for radical changes in your life. In any case, you sure will not have any children. Or even—good sex. You have to take this into account from the very beginning—you have to choose between sex and outer space, and it is an important choice, because any fucking in the world, even the most subversive fucking, is not worth the sublime and beautiful that opens up before your eyes in the field of the spaceship's searchlight; there are horizons in your life, there are landscapes that are worth paying for with the most precious thing you have, namely your erection, but to understand this, you need to be at least an astronaut, or an angel, which in the conditions of capitalism's collapse amounts to one and the same thing.

"I don't understand," I'm saying through my dream. "Why permanent fuck-all-ism?"

"Because," says Chapai, smiling happily to me from behind the transgalactic rays, "everything is a fucking waste of time: money is a fucking waste, planning systems are a fucking waste, investors are a fucking waste, the ministry is a fucking waste"—he's obviously getting worked up—"the state is a fucking waste, spheres of influence are a fucking waste, the extension of the market to the East is a fucking waste."

"The peaceful cosmos is a fucking waste," adds Vasia.

"Without a doubt," says Chapai seriously, and everyone falls silent.

*20.30*

Somewhere far-far away in the republic's east, very close to the state border, the sky smells of the early morning forest, it smells distinctively of tarpaulin tents and the pine branches that have placed their large paws on these tents. I walk along a forest path for a long-long time, on the left and the right stand tall and warm pine trees that heat up the sand around them with their breathing, and the air, and the Saturday morning forest, and the birds that appear from time to time, and in general the whole sky, and, obviously, the state border—the pines are like batteries that have put down roots right along the river, you can see the river to the left behind the trucks, and we walk along the river, we are in fact climbing, walking against the water's flow, I am six years old, I love the forest and the river, but most of all I love the weekend, I completely understand that the pines are especially warm during the weekend, and the sky is especially peaceful. I am wearing some wretched T-shirt and wretched shorts and dust-covered sandals with which I kick pine cones, raising clouds of morning dust, then the girl who is my companion turns to me and asks me to calm down and stop doing that. My companion is 16, she has agreed to go for a walk with me, in fact, my parents, who are friends with her parents, have asked her, they have all remained behind on the river beach, they are sitting there preparing salads from fresh moist vegetables, swimming in the morning river, the whole weekend lies ahead, so they are occupied with their uninteresting adult affairs, while I have found a path among the pines and my acquaintance, who does not have any particular desire to do so, it should be mentioned, has led me along this path, just so that I can finally take this walk and shut up and leave everyone alone, although she is nice to me, it would be more accurate to say that I am the one who follows her around, but she behaves quite well and does not complain about anything in particular—except that I shouldn't raise the dust or grab her hand, in short, that I shouldn't behave like a moron. I like the sand under my feet, I like the wet grass on the sand, I like the pines with the excited electrons swirling inside them, I like the noisy carefree birds on the high pine branches, I like the sky, because it reaches far-far into the distance and never ends, this I like most of all, I love it when something never ends, and the sky is one of these things, I also love it that this path never ends, it stretches forever, moving against the water's current, first drawing close to it and then curling around tree trunks, and finally my acquaintance gives in and says okay, let's take a swim and then go back, I try to bargain for one more kilometer but she says, enough, we'll swim and then go back—and I have to accept. She leaves the path and goes straight to the water, I try to keep up, following and examining her black shining bathing suit, that's the kind that was in fashion then, at the end of the seventies, her bathing suit is distinctive—there are yellow, red and orange leaves scattered on its black background, although no one, I think, swims in November, but there is a real falling of leaves on her body, and her body is beautiful and strong, these leaves suit her perfectly, even I who am six understand this, otherwise I wouldn't have followed her, the water has not had time to warm up, the bank is deserted and cool, my friend steers toward the bank and begins gradually to walk into the water, while I observe the soles of her feet disappearing under the water, her high dusky calves, her knees, her thighs, at last she falls onto the water's surface, drowning all her leaves in it—the yellow, the red, and the orange—and turns to me, come on, she shouts, come on, come on in, it's cold, I say from the bank, stop it, she shouts, it's not cold at all, come on in, she swims into the middle of the river, the current begins to carry her down and suddenly I am afraid that it will take her downstream and I will be left alone standing on this bank and of no use to anyone in front of this cold dark water that's flowing who knows where, and I can't stand it and jump into the water, forgetting that I cannot swim, and I move toward her, she notices me and begins to swim to the bank, I thrash the water with my arms, trying not to gulp water, while still in the shallow part, and finally she swims up and, breathing, out cries cheerfully, give me your hand, and I reach out my hand to her and at this moment I get a thrilling feeling, and all this water flows around me, it flows in one direction, always in one direction and I feel great, as though I'm not six but sixteen, like my friend, my big white mama, who drags me with her against the current and holds me so tightly by the hand that if I could I would simply come, but I only hang onto her and can't come, not at all, and that's how it is all my life.

"The treasury," he says, "is communal. A general treasury, created by common effort. Acronym— GT."

Having lost Vasia and myself, Chapai is desperately hanging onto his last conversational partner—Dogg.

"A workers' treasury," says Chapai. "No banks. Banks are a useless waste."

"A fiction," suggests Dogg.

"Exactly."

They remain silent for a moment, I fall asleep again, then Chapai says:

"In principle," he says. "There's a treasury here too."

Dogg looks around the room in total confusion.

"At the plant," explains Chapai. "Our director keeps it in the party committee building. The former party committee," he adds.

"So?" Dogg's ears prick up. I wake up too.

"In principle," says Chapai, "today is a holiday, the guards are only at the front gate. They walk around the territory twice every shift, and I know their route and routine."

"So?"

"In principle," explains Chapai, "it's not his money. He didn't work for it. It's labor's money. Communal."

"Like in Marx?" asks Dogg.

"Like in Marx," agrees Chapai. "We can take it."

"Are you crazy?" I say, waking up. "They'll pick you up immediately. Can't you see?" I say to Dogg, "he's gone for a ride on his PuC, he's not talking to you now, he's communicating with Karl Marx, the one of the Hamburg period."

"Don't whine so much," says Chapai, offendedly. "No one is going to pick you up. There are only two guards. This plant regularly gets robbed, including by the director. There's nothing left to steal here."

"In that case," I say, "why the devil should we poke our noses in there?"

"Today," says Chapai lowering his voice, "I saw the director packing something away in his office."

"What was it?"

"Don't know. Maybe money, maybe equipment. Some shareholders visited him, drove a microbus up and began carrying out some boxes. They completely filled the reception room and then left. But there were a few boxes left, I saw it all myself."

"Oh, right," I say, "they must be some kind of ball bearings, and we're going to risk our necks."

"They're not ball bearings at all," whispers Chapai. "If they were, he wouldn't keep them in the party committee. It's money. Or equipment. The bastard even changed the locks, I saw it with my own eyes."

"The locks?"

"The locks."

"But how will we get in there?" I ask.

"Through the roof," says Chapai. "I know a way. But we have to go now, while it's still light, and sit there on the roof until two o'clock, or until three, when the guard walks by. Then we go down and take it all out. Cleanly, without any traces."

"He will immediately suspect you," I say.

"I have an alibi," says Chapai.

"But in reality he has the clap," Dogg whispers to me, thinking that Chapai can't hear him.

*20.45*

We agree to go. Without Vasia, I say—let's do it like this: Vasia stays here to kind of keep guard, understand? he's basically part of our group and we'll count him in, but for the moment he's on guard; Vasia at this moment turns over onto his other side and falls from his chair. We pick up his exhausted body and transfer him to the sofa-bed; I look suspiciously at the covers Chapai has put there because Vasia and I still have to live together in one room, he might carry something back with him, well, okay, I think, and we go. Chapai leads us through the evening shadows across the plant, through some half-collapsed buildings in which rats scamper and birds fly, a real nature reserve, Dogg steps on some piece of metallic junk and it rings dully; quiet, hisses Chapai, carefully he leads us down some more corridors, with old newspapers and torn work clothes strewn on the floor, then we pass by the fence itself; careful, says Chapai, what is it? we ask in alarm, don't step into it, Chapai explains curtly; we carefully move through the barbed wire that has been stretched along the fence and find ourselves behind some four-storey brick building covered in new slate. Here it is, says Chapai, the party committee. Let's climb up.

Chapai goes first, since he knows the way. Before doing so he takes off his sneakers and hides them in the pockets of his sports pants, what are you doing? I say, this is for comfort, says Chapai, okay—I'm off, and he really does grab the lowest branch of the tree under the very wall, yanks himself up, sits on it, then stands up and begins to move upwards, follow me, he shouts at us from there—what? we don't understand—I say everyone follow me, repeats Chapai; the branch under him cracks and he falls straight at us, I have just enough time to jump aside and he misses Dogg too; ah, Chapai says shaking himself off, I almost made it, you go, he says to me; oh sure, I say, right now, all I need is to fall from the fourth floor on this pile of crap, come on, let's find some other way in. Well, okay, says Chapai, okay. We can just go through the door. It's not locked? I ask. I have the key, explains Chapai, I made a copy. Then why did you try to make us climb the fucking tree? I say, offended. It's more fun that way, says Chapai, and leads us to the entrance. We run across a little square, there really isn't anyone around, but as I understand it the guards can appear at any moment, Chapai quickly unlocks the door and we dive inside. Right, says Chapai, breathing fast, now upstairs, we'll wait there until night, the guards will pass by, then we'll break into the party committee. Maybe you have the keys to the party committee too? I ask hopefully, maybe we don't have to break anything? I did, says Chapai, but that bastard changed them, I told you. Why do you think I brought you with me—I won't be able to break the door down myself. Oh, I say, and I thought it was because we were your friends. The shitty Trotskyist, whisters Dogg. Enough, says Chapai resolutely, let's go upstairs, the patrol will walk by, we'll break down the door and go back, they won't pass by again until morning. And we actually get up to the fourth-floor landing. Chapai does some incantations over the lock, opens the door, we come right out on the roof, and suddenly see:

*21.00*

Many-many orange railway tracks to the west, stretching from the railway station, which is darkening to our right, and gleaming in the sun—the sun hangs over the district of Kholodna Hora; cool, I say, I'd live here if I were you, I tell Chapai, you've locked yourself up in your storeroom and are choking on various kinds of denatured alcohol, Chapai croaks confusedly, but holds onto his LSD blotter, you see that, he points to the left, what is it? I ask, examining a strange territory, scrupulously, although somewhat chaotically, filled with iron, machines, concrete, pipes, and other funny stuff, the plants, says Chapai, most of them don't work, understand, they don't work, and they did earlier? I ask just in case, I don't know this district very well, earlier they worked, says Chapai, earlier they all worked, yeah, I say, and continue to examine the railway tracks that are gradually burning out and turning dark, an endless freight train slithers out of the railway station, it's filled with sand and is crawling to the south, what's that over there? Dogg points in the direction of the freight train, that's the south, I say, see the sun on Kholodna Hora, that's the west, and the freight train is heading south, toward the sea, have you ever seen the sea? I ask Dogg, the sea? he repeats, no I haven't, in the summer I go to Saltiv, right, I say, right, you go to Saltiv and the freight trains are heading for the sea, they carry forests, what do they need forests for by the sea? asks Dogg, I don't know, to build something, what? Dogg continues to ask, the navy, Chapai suddenly says, although not quite to the point.

Dogg looks at the sun, which is beginning to dissolve over Kholodna Hora, and says, when I grow up I'll leave this place for sure, yeah? I say, and where will you go? don't know, says Dogg, south, to the sea, I'll join the navy, it's just that I can't leave my parents right now, you see, they're old, I have to look after them somehow, but in a couple of years I'll go for sure, I don't like it here—there's no work, no money, prices are high, I'll wait a couple of years and I'll leave for the south. Just try to survive the next two years, I tell him, sitting down on the sun-warmed roof.

*21.30*

Chapai advises us to sit here, no one will see us here, even if the security guard enters the party committee building, he won't come up here for sure, we'll just wait here for a few hours and then go down, it would have been harder to get here in the dark without being seen, I've thought of everything, says Chapai, today we're going to smash those capitalist pigs, stop them from getting too fat exploiting the already fucked-over proletarian masses, and we agree with him—okay, okay, if they're fucked-over than they're fucked-over, that's not our concern, we sit in silence, I say, I wonder where

Carburetor is at this moment, maybe he's already at home, sitting there, sifting his stepfather's warm ashes from hand to hand, while here we are searching for him without success, yeah, Dogg says quietly, indicating the surroundings—you won't find him here.

*22.15*

It starts to rain, the morning was sunny and warm, the air warmed up more, then the roof got hot—I thought alright , a good summer has begun—and here the rain starts up again, not a strong, real one, just a shower that wets the territory, but even so it's unpleasant, especially if you're sitting on the roof of a four-story building on the territory of a hostile plant surrounded by barbed wire, it's not much fun, I pull my old jean jacket over my head and try to fall asleep, does someone at least have a watch, I ask after a long time, we'll take our bearings from the stars, says Chapai—moron, says Dogg, referring to him; he leans against my shoulder and we try to fall asleep. From time to time I hear the voices of the freight trains in the railway station, even announcements can be heard, not from the station itself but from the train yards, their own announcements, meant only for them, they communicate with one another, it seems, only through the loudspeakers, they have a different sense of space and distance; I intermittently drift off into sleep and then back from it, as though moving from shadows to sunlight, I sink into it, as though into a warm black snow, blackest black, but warm all the same—I think, what's Yurik doing at this moment, what is he thinking about in his palace, his crucified Jesus was gold-plated and the cross itself was green. Funny, I think, maybe all the Roma have gold-plated Jesuses, maybe this is a different faith of some kind, a belief that Jesus really was gold-plated, in that case everything in this faith would be different, and their, what do you call them, prophets would have foretold the coming into the world of a little boy, a quite ordinary Eastern boy, whose physiology, or anatomy, would not differ from that of his schoolmates, except for being gold-plated, not metallic, that is, not steely and not painted but simply gold-plated, his skin must have some different atomic or cellular structure, something that has to do with the contents of the salts and calcium in the skin, some chemical stuff, I have to ask Chapai, he knows chemistry, whether there is a genetic technique for gold-plating skin, and how much this might cost the state budget.

*23.05*

Jesus cannot be gold-plated, Jesus tells me. Why can't he? I ask in wonder. It's impossible, he says, that's not the point. Then why do the Roma think that you are gold-plated? The Roma, he says, know that I am not gold-plated, they simply hide this from everyone else. Why? I say, puzzled. To distance themselves from the rest the Roma, says Jesus, are corporative, they do not need to have their faith accepted by others, understand? They specially created a gold-plated image of Jesus so that everybody would think that the Roma consider Jesus to be gold-plated. In reality they know better than everyone that I am not gold-plated. Therefore it is easier for them than for all of you, understand? I understand, I say, I understand. But all the same—why aren't you gold-plated?

But Jesus does not reply. I only see the pregnant Mary in front of me and under her skin, in her belly, the little unborn Jesus, who turns over and talks to me about something—now finally he has gone silent, it looks as though I have disappointed him, so he is simply playing under the skin of his Madonna, turning over in there like an astronaut in a state of weightlessness, touching with his lips and back and other parts of his spacesuit the thin yielding membrane that surrounds him, swimming in his mother's womb, from time to time surfacing and nudging her from within, then his little leg or knee or antennae bend Mary's body, and from under her breasts or from under her belly, as though from inside a rubber bag, Jesus pushes, knowing, unlike me, that in reality there is no body—not mine, nor Mary's, nor his own—and that all this skin has been drawn by the Roma over the fragile and painful bodies of our loves and our sufferings simply so that no one would know that no one and nothing limits us, and that we can swim wherever we like—there are no walls, there are no warnings, there is nothing that can stop you; and when he deforms her skin the next time, right under her throat, Mary laughs happily, flashing her sharp teeth, and I see how her palate is illuminated from somewhere underneath by a soft golden glow, and this golden glow mixes with the white milk in her lungs, then the glow fades and ripples, and her eyes are very, very green.

*19.06.93 (Saturday)*

*2.15*

"Listen, either we go break down the door, or we go home. I'm completely wet. Dogg looks like he's dead."

Chapai approaches Dogg and touches him squeamishly with his sneaker.

"It's okay, he's not dead," he says. "He's just fast asleep."

The rain continues to fall—fine, says Chapai, it's probably time, how do you know, I ask, by the stars? by what stars, Chapai says offended, I just heard the security guard enter about 15 minutes ago, so we can go—we wake Dogg, who at first doesn't understand where he is and who we are, but gradually he comes to his senses and we go down below.

2.25

The party committee office is on the second floor. We stand near the door, so this is how it is, explains Chapai, you—he points to me—go downstairs to the door, you—he points to Dogg—will help me, in a moment I'll find something heavy and we'll hit the door with it, forget that, says Dogg and kicks the door in with his foot—we'll be screwing around here for another half-hour, I smile with pleasure, I would have smashed it in myself, says Chapai, but I have sneakers, yeah, I add, and the clap. We quickly rifle through everything in the room: two cupboards with papers, in one there's a partially drunk bottle of cognac—Dogg immediately puts it into his pant pocket—a table with two sets of drawers as packed with various office shit as a hamburger is with cholesterol, we rummage through the stuff on the windowsill, look on the table, search for hidden compartments or at least a little safe, anything, and suddenly in the corner we see what we have been looking for—a box that used to hold xerox paper, taped and with a seal on top. The moon's gleam forces its way through the blinds on the windows and flares rapaciously on the fresh sealing wax. This is it, says Chapai. I try to lift the box, basically it's not that heavy, we can manage. So, I say, do we take it? Of course we take it, says Chapai, we take it, come on, carry it to my place, we'll look at it there. Maybe we should search some more? proposes Dogg, perhaps sensing something; no, that's all, says Chapai nervously, that's enough, let's clear out. And we walk out of the room, carefully going downstairs, Chapai does some operation with the lock, finally we end up on the street, Chapai closes up after us, and we return home—me in front with the box, Dogg behind me, and Chapai bringing up the rear, splashing through the puddles with his sneakers.

*2.55*

“Break the seal!” says Chapai to Dogg.

“What is it?” Vasia has woken up and is watching us from the couch in alarm.

“Everything’s okay,” I say, “Don’t be afraid, you’ll get your share.”

“What share?” Asks Vasia fearfully.

“You’ll see in a minute,” I say.

Among the distilling coils Dogg finds a wide kitchen knife and he cuts through the sealing wax, slowly unwinds the packaging and uncovers the contents—quicker, quicker! Chapai says impatiently, but Dogg does everything confidently and calmly, he opens the box and says—Oh, a statue! he takes out a bust about half a meter in height and puts it on the side table.

“What is it?” I say, not understanding.

“A statue,” says Dogg.

“A bust,” Chapai corrects him.

“Whose bust?” I ask.

“Ours,” says Chapai.

“That’s not what I meant—who is it?” I point at the bust.

Chapai cleans his glasses lost in thought.

“Maybe the director?” says Dogg.

“No,” says Chapai, “it’s not the director. The director doesn’t have a moustache.”

“He could have added it to improve his appearance.”

“In any case it doesn’t resemble him.”

“It’s some Marxist,” I suggest.

“Trotsky,” says Dogg. “See his nose? It’s Trotsky.”

“It’s not Trotsky,” says Chapai in irritation. “Trotsky had a beard. This one hasn’t got a beard.”

“It’s Trotsky in Mexico,” says Dogg.

"During the Hamburg period," I add.

Vasia is no help at all.

"This isn't Trotsky," Chapai begins to bluster, trying to hide his nervousness. "It's Molotov. A member of the Central Committee."

"Molotov?" I say in complete confusion.

"Molotov," says Chapai. "A member of the Central Committee," he adds just in case.

"How do you like that," I say.

Dogg morosely takes out the stolen bottle of cognac and drinks from it.

"Molotov," continues Chapai, "was the only normal guy among them. He was a hedonist. Like Tito."

"Like what?"

"Like Tito. He liked women, sports, restaurants."

"Cocktails," I say. "What's he doing at your director's?"

"They used to make them," says Chapai, after some thought, "out of waste materials. There was a special workshop here for by-products. My old man told me about it."

"Molotov's bust is what—a by-product?"

"They didn't make just Molotov's bust," Chapai justifies himself.

"What else then?"

"A bust of what's-his-name—Voroshilov. Obviously, this one survived somehow. He wanted to sell it, the bastard," says Chapai fiercely, "the people's bust."

"Listen you!" Dogg can stand it no longer. "It turns out that we broke down the door, hid from the security guards, left a whole trail, and all because of this screwy hedonist?"

Chapai walks up to him, resolutely takes the cognac out of his hands, pours the 200 grams that were left into himself, goes to the couch, pushes Vasia aside, and falls into his dirty bottomless clappy bed. Without even taking off his sneakers.

*3.30*

"So, this is what we do," says the irritated Dogg, "we take all the booze, we drain off the mash, take the dope, the rags," he looks at Chapai, "no, let him choke on his rags. We take this thing," he points at Molotov, "and we clear out before security has noticed anything."

"And what are we going to do with it?" I ask.

"We'll burn it," says Dogg. "There will be one less monster in the world."

"And Carburetor?"

"What Carburetor?" shouts Dogg. "Don't you understand? We have to clear out! Come on, let's go."

"Where to?"

"I don't know," says Dogg, "home."

"Are you planning to drag yourself across the whole town in this state?" I say. "With a bust in your arms? You'll get picked up by the first police patrol."

"Let's wait until morning," Vasia says suddenly and calmly. He has recovered his consciousness and is walking around the room, taking some brochures from the windowsill, pushing some bitten pen into his pocket, in short—he's the only one not in a panic. "In the morning we'll leave normally and no one will pick us up. The main thing is to wait it out until morning."

"Yeah," I agree, "the main thing is to wait it out."

*5.30*

I try to wake Chapai, but he just mutters in his sleep in some language of his own, the language of otherworldly Marxist-Leninists and turns away from me. Okay, I say to

Vasia, we'll leave him here, he'll have to deal with things later on his own, basically he dreamed all this up, so it's his problem, okay, says Vasia in turn, right, but we take Molotov with us, what the hell for? I say, why the hell do we need Molotov? in the first place, he'll get us arrested, explains Vasia, if they find him here in the morning Chapai will be finished, they'll figure out at once who broke down the door. In the second place, Molotov can be sold off, he's not just a lump of colored metal, he's also a sculpture, there are people who pay big money for this kind of thing. I don't know, I say, I don't know who would pay big money for Molotov, for the living one yes, but for this mummy, I point at him, well, fine, let's try to sell him off, only to whom?

Which of my acquaintances might buy Molotov's bust? This is how you establish the level of the social milieu in which you find yourself, only this way and no other. Well, I'm not familiar with any antique-dealers, jewelers, undertakers who might be able to knock the moustache off this bust and refashion it into the head of some Liudmyla Kuzminshyn Pidzaborna, who died a heroic death under the wheels of streetcar no. 5 at the intersection of Pushkinska and Vesnina Streets, and who is buried at that very spot because it was impossible to collect into a single pile everything that remained of her there at the intersection—well, I'm not acquainted with any undertakers; to continue, I'm not acquainted with any sculptors for whom this accessory material might at least have some aesthetic value, I don't have any acquaintances among communists, except for Vasia and Chapai, for whom this could become the object of a cult, I have no directors of historical museums among my acquaintances for whom this wretched hedonist might have some sort of historical value—I really don't; moreover, I'm convinced that such museum directors don't exist at all, that's what I think. So there you have it, I don't even have a place to sell off the externally quite decent-looking bust of Molotov, central committee member. Shit, why am I alive and what is my purpose? What is all this for? all this struggle for survival? this game to keep the score level? why do I need this? I'm 19 now—in five years, if I don't die from lifestyle clap, I'll still be only 24! At that age, Arkady Gaidar was no longer commanding regiments, so what about me? in principle I can do anything, well, almost anything, but here's the problem—I don't want to do anything at all! That's what comes naturally to me, although a lot of people don't understand that, that's the problem.

"Marusia!" shouts Dogg, who until this moment has been standing by the window and looking nervously into the fresh June morning. "We can sell it to Marusia—she has a whole apartment full of this kind of crap, maybe she'd like to have this monument too!" And here we all recall Mausia.

But Marusia needs to be phoned ahead of time, we can't just barge in on her—it would make things worse. Marusia is a kind of link to the external world, in fact, it was from her that I first learned that you can actually take a taxi even if you're not late for a train, or going home drunk—but just like that. You step out of your house and you need to go somewhere so you just take a taxi. And most paradoxically, you don't pay the taxi driver until the end of the journey—I also didn't know earlier that you could do that, she was the first one to show me that. And this despite the fact that she is the youngest of us all. She's only 16. Her story goes like this—her father is from the Caucasus—I don't know, he's either a Georgian or an Azeri, I think he's a Georgian, I can't tell the difference, in any case he's a general, a real general with a supply of cannon fodder in the barracks and planes in the hangars, he spent the first part of his officer's life as a nomad, traveling around the Soviet Union, defending, as I understand it, the peaceful skies of our Fatherland. He has spent the last ten years in Kharkiv, he's divorced from his wife, their only daughter eventually grew up and said to hell with both of you, the general bought her a great two-room apartment in a great building on the square, with a view of city hall, but on the top floor, under the tower itself, he either didn't have the money or enough rockets to sell so he could get something a bit closer to the ground, in any case, it's a great place. Marusia went to a top school, had a pile of money, almost gave birth a year ago at 15, her dad the general barely succeeded in persuading her to have an abortion, and even made her a present of a Zhiguli, Marusia agreed surprisingly quickly, had the abortion, ran the Zhiguli into the ground and continued to live her life, which she, with her hereditary Caucasian wisdom and love of life, divided into the beautiful and the useful—the beautiful in this case was the top school, the two-room apartment, and the beat-up Zhiguli, and the useful was all that trash and trivia with which she occupied her time free from study—Marusia knew Sasha Chernetsky, went to punk concerts, popped pills, smoked dope, drank port wine, although without dependency, which is to say that in the morning she successfully threw up the remainder of the bad alcohol and went off to study Lobachevsky or whoever it is they study in school. Paranoia, in a word, typical paranoia, we loved her for this. You could drop in on her from time to time, after phoning ahead and giving your name—she didn't remember us all, even though she'd slept with all of us, for her it wasn't sex, for her it was something much more interesting, I don't know what. We got drunk in her luxury apartment, shouted on her balcony with the view of city hall, watched her videos, and then fell asleep in her bed, sometimes even without her. In my case it wasn't even the sex so much as the possibility of at least waking up next to someone, not alone, not abandoned solely to your hangover, your own bloody nightmares, at least with somebody—that's always more fun, even if it's Marusia, who doesn't remember your name and what you did with her yesterday. She is unusually indifferent to all of us, more exactly, she would put each of us in our place each time, she seemed to be saying: the fact that you all had me yesterday only bears witness to the fact that now you'll take your barf-covered rags, all your empty containers, all your cannabis, all your personal difficulties, all your shit and clear off into your sewers, and I—Marusia—will remain here, will make myself a milk cocktail and will watch the early morning city hall, which all sorts of elected officials or just ordinary jerks will at any moment now begin entering, and this was always effective, at least it would kill me every time—invariably I would understand everything about myself that my parents never told me for some unknown reason, maybe because they just felt sorry for me.

In any case it wasn't worth going to her without phoning, you could run into the old general, although I can honestly say that I never saw him in the flesh. Marusia somehow was able to keep everything in its own place, she liked herself and her life, and obviously didn't want unnecessary flies floating around in her bouillon, besides that the old man himself probably suspected that his darling daughter Marusia sometimes failed to observe the garrison's internal regimen, therefore, when he wanted to visit his child, he also always phoned her ahead of time, that's their Caucasian custom, then she would throw all her casual guests out of the window, force them to take with them all their empty containers and unfinished boiled kovbasa, she threw the cigarette ends out the little window, tossed the bongs into the trash, poured the crumbs into the toilet bowl—in short, took down all the decorations and returned to her normal life with her dad the general, the republic's armed forces, regular meals, gyms, tennis courts, decent friends, higher education, nice music—meaning nice live music, not recordings, although there are nice recordings, too—in short, all that minimal collection of artificial limbs and false jaws that has been made to transport you more comfortably through your life, provided for you by the system, on condition that you agree in your will to transfer to its name your kidneys, lungs, sexual organs, and soul. She had all these artificial limbs, so she could allow herself to go wild and occasionally to climb down pretty deeply into society's sewage tunnels, to fly for a couple of twenty-four hour periods to the other side of the moon, which all the time was located not too far from here—to spend some time there feeding on grass and port wine, to join for a time the Great Nervous System, the Torn and Patched Network of Blood Circulation and Love, to sink her head into the flow of lymphs, excrement, and sperm at the very bottom of which, some people think, can be found the greatest concentration and most wonderful chunks of happiness, although really there is nothing there, you can take it from me.

*6.00*

So we would have been sure to phone her, if we could have found a phone, but it turned out that the nearest telephone was in the regional militia office, where guards with scimitars and flame-throwers were waiting for us, with hand grenades and anti-personnel mines carefully buried in the factory flower beds, in short—I wouldn't go there, especially carrying a moustachioed Molotov, better to take everything we need—we tell each other—and we collect all the booze and the rest of the dope, Vasia even takes some brochures from the windowsill—and we climb over the fence. I also say, maybe—I say—we should leave a note for Carburetor, so he'll know where to find us, but Vasia says skeptically that this wouldn't be a note for Carburetor but for the district attorney, so really why should we make more trouble for ourselves, now that things have turned out this way, we have to get out of this situation with dignity, there's no other way. Chapai continues to turn around his own axle in bed, as though someone was rotating him in his dreams, like some sort of fly-wheel, and trying to set in motion something very important for the world but it just wasn't working: however the fly-wheel got turned, nothing came of it, this exhausted and sick body would continue to hurt as though a splinter had been inserted by diabolical artillery men into the rear end of Marxism-Leninism and left there as a reminder of one more lost soul.

*6.15*

We walk through the morning in the private sector, come out onto the same square by the circus, I am carrying the moustachioed Molotov and Dogg the booze, naturally we didn't drain off the mash, but we kept our own three cognacs, the ones we extracted honestly from Uncle Robert; Vasia isn't carrying anything, he feels the worst, in any case he says so, and we have no evidence to disbelieve him. We only have to cross the bridge, turn toward the church, crawl through several blocks and come out on the square, then cross the street again and jump into the entrance of the building with the tower, and if we are lucky enough not to be stopped, our lives will continue happily for several more hours, until lunch for sure.

*6.45*

Marusia has colored her hair again. Her real hair color is, I think, black, I'm almost sure it's black, this would be natural, she's from the Caucasus after all, now she has colored it some kind of dark red and cut it very short, she is wearing a black dressing gown, and there's nothing underneath except Marusia herself, she flings all of this out at us, we are already in a bad state and now we have to deal with this. Who are you? she first asks us, then she recognizes Vasia, she never recognizes me, I have even given up being offended by this, and Dogg has no pretensions whatsoever, well—she says—what have you brought? she is still asleep, standing right there in the corridor, she's standing and sleeping, but talks to us about something, badly, to be sure, but at least she's saying something, and it's good that she let us in; what have you brought? she asks again, what have we brought? Vasia asks in puzzlement, yes, you promised, says Marusia, I tense up, there's something wrong here, maybe we should take off right away and not wait for the next unpleasantness from the general's staff, you just phoned, says Marusia, half-asleep, and I asked for some; that wasn't us who phoned, says Vasia, not you? she says in amazement, not us, what is it you need? asks Vasia, we have everything, can we sit here for a while? Marusia lowers her shoulders in disappointment, as though to indicate sit down, what do I care, she turns around and disappears into her room and we are left in the corridor with our friend Molotov, the central committee member.

"Somehow she doesn't seem pleased to see us," says Dogg and goes into the kitchen.

"She's not pleased with anyone," I say, following him. "Why should she be pleased."

"Well, and why not," says Dogg, pouring the cognac into coffee mugs. "If someone brought me three bottles of cognac in the morning, I'd be overjoyed."

"If someone brought me," say I, drinking, "Molotov's bust, I'd have to think whether I should be overjoyed."

"We have to wake her," says Dogg, pouring a new round. "Because it's not right somehow—here we are visitors, sitting around, boozing."

"Yes, it's not right," I say. "But not boozing would be better. We'd do better to get some sleep ourselves. This is already the second night I can't get some normal sleep. First the cop station, then that Marxist in sneakers. I want to sleep. Let's go to sleep."

"Sleep?" asks Dogg. "You know, right now I'm in such a state that I'm simply afraid to sleep."

"Why afraid?" I ask.

"I'm afraid that if I fall asleep I won't have the presence of mind to wake up, understand?"

Dogg pours again, but I refuse, that's it, I say, enough, let's go to bed, Dogg gets up with displeasure, on the sofa in one of the rooms we find Vasia, who has wrapped himself in some blanket and is sleeping contentedly, and there's nothing left for us but to go and find some other bed or sofa, or something, we go into the other room and see Marusia there in the large bed that is very familiar to us, now without even the dressing gown, she has pushed her head under the pillow and is sleeping that way and is not paying us any particular attention, this is a strange endless night that is now transforming into a similar morning, our friends crawl off into various corners and lose contact with one another at this time, it's as though they die every morning at 7:00 am, it looks like that at any rate, if not more terrifying. That's it, I'm going to sleep, I say to Dogg, he walks up to the bed, move over, he says to Marusia and pushes her to the edge of the bed, you can sleep here—he says to me—no, I say, you sleep by her—why me? asks Dogg—and why me? I say—you want to sleep, don't you, and me—he says—I'm afraid of her. I sigh and agree, but all the same I place Molotov between myself and Marusia, just in case.

*9.57*

"Oh, hell!" she cries out. "What's that?!"

I wake up and look around in fear. Next to me on the bed sits Marusia, completely naked, covering herself with the pillow and looking at me in fear.

"Hell!" she cries. "Oh, hell! What's that?"

"Don't shout," I say, trying to calm her. "Why are you shouting?"

"What is that?" she says, pointing at the bust and holding the pillow with the other hand. Dogg has also woken up and run off to the door. Marusia must have frightened him.

"It's a bust," I tell her. "Don't shout."

"Hell!"

"What of it?" I say in fear. "A bust. It's just a bust. We brought it."

"What for?" Marusia asks suspiciously.

"For no particular reason," I say. "We thought maybe you could use it."

"I don't need it," she says nervously.

"Okay, then we'll take it away in a moment."

"How did you get in here?" asks Marusia.

"You let us in yourself," I say, confused.

"Why?"

"I don't know," I say. "We came, you let us in."

"Did you bring some?" asks Marusia, obviously remembering something.

"What?" I say, not understanding.

"Well, anything."

"Here," I say. "We brought Molotov."

"What Molotov?" she asks puzzled.

"The central committee member."

"Where is he?" asks Marusia, failing to understand.

"Well, here," I point at Molotov.

Marusia attempts to grasp something. Then she takes a cigarette from somewhere and a lighter and begins to smoke, nervously thinking everything through.

"Have you been here long?" she asks.

"Not very," I say. "About two or three hours."

"I see," she says.

I sit with her in her bed and we look at one another silently. She is nice-looking, she drinks too much but she's still nice-looking. Especially with the pillow.

"You want to smoke?" I ask.

She picks up her cigarette and shows me, as if to say. I am smoking.

"We brought some," I say.

"You brought some?" she suddenly wakes up. It's as though a password has been given, in any case the right combination of words that sets everything in motion. The whole thing even appeals to me, so I repeat it:

"Yes," I say, "we brought some."

"Hell," says Marusia, and looking fearfully at Molotov she puts the pillow in its place.

*10.15*

In the morning it's better to not look at such things at all, or, if one has to look, then only superficially. That's what I do, and while she is walking around the room and finding her panties and socks, pulling on her torn designer jeans, putting on various medals and bracelets, I go onto the balcony and wait for her there. She comes out with a big black pipe, and after that we just stand on the balcony and talk about almost nothing, just look at the storm clouds in the morning sky; at the city hall, empty on a Saturday, there is so much air and dampness in all this that I get the feeling we are in someone's lungs, for example, the lungs of an old flounder who has swallowed icy arctic waves and is now lying at the bottom of the ocean, silently suffering from an overdose.

"How are things?" I ask. We saw each other a week ago, it was very cold, we phoned her from the railway station, but what were we doing at the railway station? I cannot remember now, but we phoned her for sure from the station, she said—okay, come on over, just bring some booze, we picked up a bottle of Kaiser, then walked over, she had just been to some massage parlour and smelled of some kind of creams, her hair was a bit longer and, as I recall, a different color, although I can't remember which color.

"Things are bad," she says.

"What happened?"

"It happened," she says. "Things happened. Problems at school. I flunked the exam."

"Cool," I say. "You go to school."

"There's nothing cool about it," says she. "It's completely shitty."

"I see."

"We had to write a paper," says Marusia, warming the pipe in her hands. "You know what the topic was?"

"What?" I ask.

"What I think of city services."

"What's that?"

"City services?"

"Yeah."

"You know, firemen, let's say. Or the gas service. Communal services, in a word."

"I see. And what did you write?"

"I wrote about the street watering trucks."

"What trucks?"

"Watering trucks. The ones that wash the streets in the mornings, have you seen them?"

"Yes," I say. "Do you know something about watering trucks?"

"I had spent a terrible night. Almost no sleep. Came to class and my body was just falling apart, you see? I almost died."

"Well, you should have gone home."

"It was an exam."

"Should have asked dad, he would have sent a couple of armored personnel carriers and solved the problem."

"That's easy for you to say. Your dad's not in the military."

"Yeah," I say, "thank God."

"Actually, he really likes it when I ask him something like that. That's why I never ask him."

"Ah," I say.

"Brother's always milking him."

"He has a brother?"

"I have a brother," Marusia says, finally lighting the pipe. "An older brother."

"Why have I never seen him?"

"I don't allow him here."

"Why?"

"I hate him. Though before I loved him very much."

"And what happened?"

"He hit on me."

"Seriously?"

"Seriously. Once he almost raped me, it's a good thing he was smoked up—he just couldn't do anything. Otherwise, imagine, he could have been my first man."

"Yeah," I say, "it happens. My brother used to stick up for me when I was a kid."

"No one touched me when I was a child," she says. "They were afraid ..."

*11.00-12.00*

"And so?"

"What?"

"You were saying something about street watering trucks."

"Oh, yes," she remembers. We are sitting on the balcony, Dogg is sleeping in the corner, and we are sitting on some carpets and looking into the sky, Marusia is completely lost, she looks around with empty eyes, trying to grasp onto anything at all, she has trouble doing this, but now she has turned her attention to me and she is trying to say something. "I had a vision. I hadn't slept the previous night, you see, and then there was this assignment to write. In a word, I wrote something along the lines of, I don't remember exactly now, but the main idea was that in reality those watering trucks aren't full of water at all."

"What, then?"

"You see," her voice has turned serious and frightened, "I woke up one morning, very early, before six, I think, and something inside me insisted that I need to buy milk, and so I picked up the thermos and went off in my slippers to find milk."

"At six in the morning?"

"I didn't know," she says, "that it was only six. I simply walked out onto the balcony and it was light out, I looked down—below these machines were driving by, you know—the watering trucks, I thought for some reason that they were milk trucks, they look a bit like them, don't you think?"

"Well, not exactly."

"Why?"

"Where have you seen milk trucks pouring milk onto the street?"

"Milk?" Here Marusia turns silent, obviously having another vision, but I succeed in pulling her back.

"Although," I say, "they really are a bit like them. The principle is the same. They are carrying something around in tanks. Fire-engines are a bit like them too."

"And gasoline trucks," says Marusia.

"Yeah," I say, "fuel trucks look basically like milk trucks too."

"Then I went up to a watering truck with my thermos," Marusia goes on, "and here, you know, a stream of water hit me, it landed right on me, my body, my face, my arms, it even knocked the thermos out of my hands. And then I raised my hands to my face, cold water was running down them, and I smelled them. You know what they smelled of?"

"What?" I ask.

"Gas."

"What gas?"

"I don't know," says Marusia. "But it was a gas, for certain. And you know what I thought, that this could basically be deliberate, you understand—they deliberately add gas as a tonic to the water for watering, maybe on the one hand to stimulate the population before the working day, and on the other hand to direct this same population's energy in a productive direction, because this gas was basically made out of psychotropic stuff, to make people turn on their engines, so to speak, and cheerfully go off to their workplace."

"And you wrote all this down?"

"Yes," says Marusia, "I did. I was having a vision. I also began dreaming up various variations on this theme, such as, for example, that all the elements in this gas, when they find their way into the air, begin to act only after 45 minutes. And if the water trucks sent the gas into the air at 6:15 a.m., it would be only partially activated before 7:00 and would in fact be extremely harmful for the human body."

"Why is that?"

"To regulate the daily timetable in the cities. If you stick your nose out into the street before 7:00, you get your share of harmful liquid and have cramps all day, get it? But if, instead, you leave the house at, say, exactly 7, you get the normal dose of the mixture and cheerfully spend the whole day working for the fatherland, that way everything is economical and rational."

"And you wrote about that too?"

"Uh-huh."

"You know," I say, "if I were you, I would talk to your dad all the same. A couple of armored personnel carriers, and no one would ever learn about that gas in the water… Or just one hydrogen bomb," I add after some thought.

*12.00-13.00*

"No," she says, "I'll just rewrite it. I'll write about something else. For example, about the streetcar depot."

"I can just imagine your essay! Listen," I say, "we have a real problem here. Our friend's parents have died."

"Both?" asks Marusia.

"No," I say. "Only one. The stepfather."

"And who's your friend?"

"Carburetor. Remember him?"

"What's he like?

"Well," I say, "he has a funny face, far-eastern. High cheekbones, narrow eyes—remember?"

"He's the one who looks Chinese?"

"More Mongolian," I say.

"What's the difference?"

"Mongolians are illiterate."

"And the Chinese?"

"The Chinese were literate before the Mongols appeared."

"Yes," says Marusia, "I remember him. You brought him along once. And now what?"

"Well," I say, "now we have to find him. The funeral is tomorrow. And there's no sign of him. Can you imagine?"

"Yes," says Marusia, "it's a mess. What did you say his name was?"

"Carburetor."

"Strange name."

*13.00-14.00*

"Carburetor?"

"Right."

"Listen," Marusia finally lifts her head and looks at me more or less consciously. "Is that the guy whose father died?"

"Stepfather."

"One and the same dick," says Marusia, waking up fully. "Yesterday your friend phoned me, the pudgy, dirty one."

"Cocoa," I say.

"What?"

"That's what we call him—Cocoa."

"What a nightmare," she says. "He phoned yesterday looking for you guys."

"He phoned you?"

"Well, who should he phone?" Marusia tries to get up on her feet. "He was looking for you, talked precisely about your—what did you call him?…"

"Carburetor."

"Right, Carburetor. He said, I think, that he knows where he is."

"Where is he?"

"Carburetor?"

"No, not Carburetor?" I say, getting up too, "this fat jerk."

"He's at Gosha's. That's where he phoned from."

"Who's Gosha?"

"What's the matter with you?" she asks. "Where do you live? Gosha's the editor of our trendiest newspaper. This beast, if I am not mistaken, works for him," says Marusia, pointing at the sleepy Dogg.

"Is he the editor or what?" Finally I'm beginning to get it.

"Right, what do you think I'm talking about?"

"How did our Cocoa end up there?"

"How should I know?" says Marusia and goes out of the room

"Wait!" I call after her. "Do you know his phone number?"

"No," calls Marusia from somewhere in the kitchen. "I know the address. I slept with him a few times, at his place. He has a big apartment, not far from here, on Gogol Street. He lives there alone."

"Wait, just a minute." I find Marusia in the kitchen—she looks in the fridge, gets out a jar of honey, falls into a chair, and begins to eat. "Wait," I repeat, "what else did he tell you?"

"What else?" Marusia thinks for a moment. "Nothing else. He said that he knows where your ... well, the one whose father died ... rather, stepfather. Said that when you want, you can find him at Gosha's."

"How did he end up there?!"

"Well, and how should I know!" Marusia can't take any more and begins to shout. "How should I know? Maybe Gosha picked him up somewhere and had him!"

"What do you mean, picked him up and had him?" I say, not understanding.

"Silently! Saw him and picked him up and silently fucked him. Don't you know Gosha?"

"No."

"Gosha is a class-A jerkoff in this wretched town. That's how he recruits his editorial team. I slept with him on principle too, that was kind of my principle. So, maybe he picked your stinker up somewhere, fucked him, and is now supporting him at his place on Gogol Street, I don't know." She falls silent and continues to lick her hot-yellow cold honey.

*14.15*

"Listen, we're off."

"Uh-huh," she says.

"Give me Gosha's address."

Marusia takes out some notebook covered in yellow leather, writes something in it, tears out a page, and passes it to me. Here, she says, only you have to ring for a long time, the apartment is large, he can be sleeping and simply not hear you. You can say that I sent you, otherwise he might not let you in, understand? I understand, thanks, well, alright—get out, she says and immediately forgets us. We are on our way out, and here—in the doorway—I turn to her and say:

"Marusia," I say. "Listen, there's another thing."

"What?"

"Maybe you'd like to take our Molotov?"

"Molotov?" she asks.

"Well, yeah, Molotov. It's tough for us to drag him around all the time, and maybe you'd like him. He was, after all, a central committee member."

Marusia walks up to me, examines Molotov, runs her hands over his face, and says:

"Okay. I'll take him. I like him—he looks like my dad. He has the same bullshit on his jacket."

"It's not bullshit," I say. "It's the order of Lenin."

Okay, says Marusia, to hell with you—here's some money—she shoves me a note, let me drive you, or else you'll get arrested outside the entrance, put—she tells me—put Molotov on the balcony, he's mine now, I obediently carry Molotov onto the balcony, and we go downstairs; Marusia leads us to the garage, the garage door is reinforced with iron and copper, genuine gates of hell, you could hide dragons behind these doors, or nuclear bombers, something apocalyptic at any rate. It's funny, but Marusia only has her run down Zhiguli in there, the garage door contains another door, a smaller one, covered in steel in the same way, Marusia opens it, come in, she says, maybe, says Vasia, we should open the garage door? You come in, says Marusia, I'll open the garage myself, otherwise someone might see you hanging around the garage—they'll start asking questions, I'll do it myself, get in the car, we walk into a dark garage, and in fact see the beat-up but still fully battle-ready Zhiguli there and the three of us—me, Vasia the Communist, and Dogg Pavlov—squeeze into the back seat, Dogg at first wants to sit in front, but the right door is broken and bent inwards, so we take Dogg in with us, on our knees, so to speak. Marusia stands by the garage door for a while, finds an unfinished cigarette somewhere in the pocket of her jeans, finishes it off quickly and remembers that she has forgotten something, what have I forgotten, she thinks, what? why am I standing by the garage, probably I wanted to drive somewhere, but where? she thinks, and pensively walks inside and sits by the wheel, well,

Marusia, Dogg calls to her nervously, are we off? we're off, Marusia reacts to the challenge, she turns on the engine and puts the car in reverse. She has, of course, forgetten to open the garage door.

*14.45*

"Can you get out?" I ask.

"I can get out, I can get out," says Marusia. "Everything's okay."

"Go home," Vasia says to her. "Can you make it on your own?"

"I can make it," says Marusia.

"Are you sure?" asks Vasia.

"Uh-huh," she says and tries to start the engine again.

Vasia leans over from the back seat and takes the keys from her. We drag our friend out of the driver's seat, close up the garage after ourselves, put the keys in her hands and go off, thinking—will she be okay or not, and if she ends up okay, where will that be? But it turns out that while we're walking to the square and looking up at the building opposite city hall, Marusia miraculously appears on her balcony, she's already sitting there, pressed against Molotov—two unfortunate, wasted creatures, Marusia in her torn designer jeans and Rolling Stones T-shirt, and Molotov, central committee member, old hedonist, lover of cocktails, now closer to the heavens, maybe only by a few meters, but closer.

*Part Two*

## THE RIVER THAT FLOWS AGAINST ITS OWN CURRENT

*15.15*

I press for a long time and insistently, I have no choice, what can you do in such a situation—if he's not in we'll have to return home, and who knows what awaits us there, in that case this whole plot has been pointless, why have we dragged ourselves around town for two days, trying to make something out of this messy situation, so the whole thing is ... he better be here, but no one opens the door, and I'm already thinking, well, fine, it didn't work out, they'll bury the stepfather and that will be the end of it, our friend will travel for the forty-days after service, if they really need him that badly, they can make a record of everything, photograph his ashes, or take a video, so that a grief-stricken Carburetor can later view the sad ceremony during long winter evenings before going to sleep. Dogg finally cannot stand it and begins kicking the door, I try to calm him, but some shuffling can be heard behind the door, someone, it seems, is coming toward us, the door really does open and a bald fat guy in a blue silk dressing gown comes out.

"Whachawant?" he asks.

"We want Cocoa," Dogg tells him.

In silence the guy takes an air pistol from his dressing gown pocket and points it at Dogg's mug.

"What cocoa?" he asks.

"Our friend," says Dogg in fright. "Cocoa."

"What's your game?" says the agitated guy, who's obviously Gosha.

Vasia hides behind my back, and I'm thinking—what's he called, our Cocoa—what's he called, what can a Donbas intellectual possibly be called? probably Andriusha, that's it—Andriusha.

"Andriusha," I say. "We need Andriusha. We're his friends."

"Yeah?" Gosha is distrustful. "Well, okay, come in," he says without putting the pistol away. Suddenly he notices Dogg's backpack and says: "What's in there?"

"Booze," says Dogg.

"Let's have it," says Gosha.

Dogg takes out a bottle of cognac, gives it to Gosha, who silently puts it in his dressing gown pocket, we follow him and emerge into an enormous room, the corridor leads somewhere into the depths, we walk behind Gosha and enter a limitless kitchen, he has it not fucking bad, obviously people pay him for spitting on our holy shrines, I think enviously, Cocoa is sitting in the kitchen, without his suit, to be sure, also in some dressing gown, I get the impression that they have some sort of sauna here, he's sitting there drinking something from a big mug, maybe it's precisely cocoa that he's drinking, Andriusha, it's your friends, says the jerkoff-editor to him and, losing all interest in us, disappears in the thickets of his jerkoff apartment.

"Greetings," Cocoa smiles at us joyfully, the fat moron.

"Greetings, Cocoa," says Vasia. "Cool dressing gown. Are you going to wear it everywhere now?"

"Gosha gave it to me," explains Cocoa.

"Well, fine," I interrupt him. "Marusia said that you phoned, something about Carburetor."

"Oh, right," says Cocoa. "I wanted to tell you yesterday, but you wouldn't listen."

"What are we going to listen to you for," begins Dogg, but Vasia restrains him, indicating, as it were, let him speak.

"So," continues Cocoa joyfully, "you went and then I got to thinking I should warn you somehow."

"Warn us about what?" asks Vasia.

"About Carburetor."

"You know where he is?"

"Yes."

"Is he in town?"

"What are you, total losers?" Cocoa begins to show bravado, feeling that he's on his own territory after all, the moron. "Okay, they're jack-asses, but you Zhadan ought to know, you're in school with him aren't you?"

"I've been ill," I say.

"Uh-huh," he agrees, "that's going to last a long time. Carburetor has been in the camp for a while."

"What camp?" I ask in terror.

"What's happened, have they put him away?" Dogg also takes fright.

"No, not that, where would they put him?" laughs Cocoa. "He's in this pioneer camp, or whatever they're called these days, a laboring class camp, that's what they call them. Right now is their first, what's it, session, no not session, intake. No, not intake, rotation. A pile of underaged jerks arrive, and Carburetor teaches them how to put up a tent."

"You don't say," I say in wonder.

"Yeah," Cocoa tells us, "it's cool in the camp. A whole bunch of girls. I once went there when I was still in school, some group leader hit on me—turns out he's a fag."

"Now Carburetor is probably hitting on someone," says Vasia.

"Is he a fag too?" Dogg fails to understand.

"No, Carburetor isn't a fag," I say. "I know him well. Although in his own way he's a fag, sure."

"Well, what do we do?" Vasia asks Cocoa.

"Go see him," says Cocoa. "There are some classy girls there."

"And jerkoff group leaders," adds Dogg.

"And where is this?" asks Vasia.

"Past Vuzlova," says Cocoa. "Camp Chemist."

"What is it, a camp for mutants?" I ask.

"No, it's for chemists. So, you catch the electric train and drive across Chuhuiv to the last stop, Kintseva. There you wait a couple of hours for the next electric train and travel to Vuzlova. There you wait another couple of hours and ride to Chemist. From Vuzlova you can even walk it. But you need to set off at night, otherwise you won't make it. The first electric train is at four in the morning. You'll get there just before lunch. You can booze in Chuhuiv," he adds for some reason.

"How's that, on the fly?" asks Vasia the Communist.

"Well, however you like," Cocoa replies discontentedly. Obviously he has some fixed idea about Chuhuiv, sometimes that happens.

*16.00*

"What if we set out right now?" I ask just in case.

"The last electric train is at half past four, I think," explains Cocoa. "You won't make it. Take the night train," he smiles.

"What are you smiling for?" I ask him in displeasure. "Why are you smiling, eh?"

"No reason," Cocoa says in confusion. "Just so."

"Just so," I say in displeasure.

"Enough," says Vasia, "can we sit here until evening? Or are you going to start screwing in a moment?"

"I'll ask Gosha," say the embarrassed Cocoa.

"About what?" asks Vasia, but Cocoa is already walking out.

"What a moron," Dogg says unhappily after he leaves.

*16.15*

"Gosha said that you can sit here," Cocoa rushes into the kitchen joyfully. "Just be more careful in the toilet."

"Hear that, Dogg?" says Vasia. "More careful in the toilet. Everything the same, only more careful."

"Sit down," says Cocoa, waving the sides of his dressing gown. "Want some tea?"

"Do you have any vodka?" asks Vasia.

"No, there's no vodka. Gosha doesn't drink."

"Uh-huh, he doesn't drink," says Dogg, "but he took the cognac."

"We still have a bottle left," I say.

"I don't want cognac," says Vasia. "I get heartburn from it. Come on," he says to Dogg, "why don't you go buy some vodka. I think I still have some money left."

Vasia takes the rest of his profits and gives them to Dogg. Cocoa closes the door after him, will you find your way back? he asks on the doorstep, no problem, says Dogg and disappears. And we are left behind to wait for him.

*16.30-18.00*

"Maybe he died?"

"Maybe he did," says Vasia. "Or maybe he just took off with my money."

"Drop it," I say. "Don't you know Dogg? He hasn't run off."

"That means he died," says Vasia.

"I'm going," Cocoa says timidly, he's also been sitting here with us here for half an hour, feeling sad but not leaving, in the end he breaks down and says—I'm going."

"Where to?" I ask.

"Well," Cocoa points to the corridor, "there. You can sit here. You can make some tea. If you need me just call."

"Go on then," Vasia says after him. "Listen," he says to me, "how did he get here?"

"Don't know," I say. "How did we get here? You see what's happening to the world."

"Where's Dogg?" Vasia keeps repeating.

*18.45-19.10*

"Maybe he's been crushed by something?"

"Maybe. By a streetcar. Or killed by a current."

"What kind of current?"

"Electric."

"Better a streetcar, then."

*19.30*

"I think I have some dope left."

"So why didn't you say anything?"

"I forgot," says Vasia, and he really does find the rest of the grass in his jeans. That's it then, the money is finished, this is the last of the grass, a natural cycle has been completed, there's no other word for it. A complete natural cycle," says Vasia to me and rolls a joint.

*19.30-21.30*

We don't even have anything to recall. We sit in silence, focused on something or other and suddenly begin noticing all these things around us, you know, the old kitchen, let's say, someone probably lived there before him, I'm always blown away by these things—it's just that the places in which I lived as a rule were not much older than I was, they could have been built in my lifetime, while here there's some kind of furniture, a mountain of dirty dishes, he lives like an animal, doesn't clean up after himself at all, if he was a maniac, they would be able to catch him by the remains of the bodies in his tin cans in the kitchen, and here I'm thinking—why didn't I get an apartment like this, I would keep it clean and tidy, wouldn't allow any retards, and wouldn't even come here myself—for the purity of the experiment I would close the door, seal the lock and to hell with everyone—a singular example of exemplary living, when I become a full representative of this fucked-up society, I'll start buying up real estate, renovating it, bringing it up to human standards and sealing it, there has to be internal order, not an intentional one, apartments are like the circus—all the shit has to be cleaned up, otherwise you'll never have enough time to remove the corpses, his place smells of coffee and ketchup, the sweet smell of ketchup, the smell of a good life and regular meals, I can't stand it, the ketchup gets under my skin, I sniff my nails—they smell of ketchup—ketchup and coffee powder, honey and ketchup, all these pots and ladles, large plates smeared with omelette, and forks with dried chocolate on them—it all smells of ketchup, I start to fell nauseous, and I say to Vasia let's get out of here, where to? he says, where would we go? it's dark outside, it's still too early for us, we need to wait here and then we can go, let's wait at the jerkoff's, ketchup—I say, what? Vasia fails to hear me, ketchup—I shout to him, and he nods his head as though trying to say uh-huh, ketchup-

ketchup, definitely ketchup, let's go into the other room, I say, there's a lot of dishes here, he doesn't object, and we go into the corridor and enter the living room, his living room is also packed with all sorts of antique shit, this always irritates me, in the sense of seeing that someone already lived here before me and in contrast to me lived a real life—ate breakfasts, had sex, maybe even loved someone, visited the markets and stores, bought not what he could but what he wanted, ketchup, had a job, communicated with various people, wore glasses that he liked, took vacations, real vacations, went on picnics, knew how to cook, cooked various tasty dishes and even ate them, ketchup, ketchup, when he was sick he treated himself not just with vodka but had various medicines, a home drugstore, doctor-acquaintances, during lunch breaks he could enter the restaurant, not just to have a drink but to eat, had a favorite dish, favorite fucking spices, ketchup, ketchup, ketchup, and where was I all this time? why wasn't I here among all these cupboards and couches covered in ketchup and lemon juice, why did no one adopt me, let's say, when I lived for several days at the bus station and slept on wooden chairs, or when I lived off boiled water for several days, come to think of it why doesn't anyone adopt me now, why doesn't this jerkoff adopt me? I would be the jerkoff's regimental son, I'm 19, I'm already able to take care of myself, I don't need constant attention, I don't need to have my diapers changed and don't need to be fed porridge—yes, some minimal nourishment, warm water, toilet paper, porn videos, girls in the kitchen, hemp on the balcony, but even this isn't the main thing, the main thing is to have some fatherly attention, normal and constant fatherly attention, real fatherly attention, like on television.

We find a cool radiola, I used to have one like that in my childhood—on four high legs, in a wooden case with a glass screen on which you can read the names in red of all the cities under the sun, cities that I dreamed of in my childhood and which could hear me—Prague, Warsaw, Belgrade, East Berlin, on a cool radiola like this you can listen to vinyl and radio, in my childhood I listened to scratched vinyl, but this jerkoff doesn't have vinyl, to be sure he does have some old Soviet Beatles, but what are Vasia and I—total losers, to listen to the Beatles, and in this hallucinatory state when things fall apart and scents, by contrast, stick together, and it's simply impossible to make sense of it all, we begin to turn the dial on the radio, the cool radiola crackles sadly, and suddenly we hear a voice from the other side:

Good evening, dear radio listeners. May harmony descend on your quiet abodes.

"May who descend?" Vasia asks.

"Harmony," I say. "On abodes."

"Ah," says Vasia.

Today, with you on this marvelous evening

"Oh, yeah," says Vasia, "marvelous evening: the rain has been pissing down all day."

As always on Saturdays at 22:00 the youth program Musical Partners and I—your host khrrrrrrr khrrrrrrrr—says the radio. Today's broadcast of our program will be entirely dedicated to the creativity of the popular Irish musical group, known not only in our country but in other European countries—the band Depeche Mode. Your questions and thoughts can be expressed by telephoning khrrrrr khrrrrrr khrrrrrrrrr—says the host.

"What a cool program," say I.

"Yeah," says Vasia, "better than the Beatles."

And while you are asking your questions, we will play an instrumental composition of stepan haliabarda called "A Letter to Mama."

The composition really does begin, and immediately drives us insane, this stepan haliabarda puts so much hallucinogen into his synthesizer, the sound is so terrible, that it can't fail to drive you insane, they probably deliberately hired to work on the radio, just so they can mess things up and drive listeners out of their minds after five seconds of their musical compositions, just so that he—this incredible and unreal stepan haliabarda—can touch the plastic of his synthesizer with his soft hairy fingers—and snap—your guts start turning inside out and you're transformed into a weapon of the Lord's providence and cannot move from the radio until they give you the weather forecast, we sit under our cool radiola, with our backs against it and lean on one another, so as not to fall to the sides, we examine the chairs, cupboards and couches, do you notice, I say, how it smells of lemons here? I notice, says Vasia, of lemons and cats. Not cats, I say, not cats—ketchup. Cats, he disagrees. And ketchup, I add.

This has been an instrumental composition of stepan haliabarda entitle "A Letter to Mama," says the cosmic radio host. It was performed by the author. And our program today, I remind you, is dedicated to the work of the well-known Irish group Depeche Mode. The program is based on the research in David Bascombe's documentary *God as Heroin,* published this year in the British Isles and lovingly translated and sent to us by our London editors. And so, Depeche Mode (a musical insert can be heard, I suspect by the same stepan haliabarda, because we turn into zombies again). The work of these lads from Ulster has long been popular with our youth. So what is the secret of the success enjoyed by these completely unknown boys, who grew up in the very centre of Ireland's cesspool? Together with you, our dear radio listeners, we will try to find an answer. As biographers affirm, on one grey autumn morning in 1962 in an Ulster port occupied by the British colonialists (stepan haliabarda adds a tragic note from his synthesizer, heavily pressing the plastic with his soft little fingers) a boy was unexpectedly born to the family of a simple Irish sailor and a printer, Ben and Mary Han. The parents reacted with concern to the birth because this was already their fifth child, the previous four, as Mr. Bascombe affirms, died a sudden death at an early age from a difficult type of intestinal infection that is widespread in the poorest districts of Ulster closest to the ports. Obviously a similar unenviable fate awaited the Hans' fifth son—the hard conditions of life under occupation did not give his parents reasons to hope for something positive for their wretched surviving child. They decided to call their little boy Dave in honor of Saint Dave, who, as is well-known, is the patron of Irish partisans and a symbol of this small—as compared to us—people in its struggle with British colonialists. In the core Irish population there are many popular legends and beliefs associated with Saint Dave, in particular, he is known in ancient Irish epics as the god of cattle, milking and simply fertility. Even to this day Irish football fanatics, when going to the stadium to support their beloved team collectively sing "Saint Dave, fuck the Catholic devils today." Dave's father, the old goggle-eyed Ben, had long been known for his support of the IRA and gave the cantor regular and secret contributions to the army from his miserable naval salary.

"It this the Beatles now?" Vasia asks.

Dave's mom worked in the offices of a port printing house, and risked her life and reputation by occasionally helping the insurgents to alter their driving and marriage licenses. In this way the young Dave grew up in a nationally conscious atmosphere, hating the Queen Mother, Prince Charles and all the latter's underaged progeny, at least this is what Mr. Bascombe affirms. The future performing artist's first emotional impressions were associated with an event during the forcible dispersal throughout the Catholic areas of a First of May demonstration—traditional for Irish separatists—

mounted British police raped Dave's dad ... no—the host suddenly stumbles—not his dad. His mom. Yes—Dave's mom. Excuse me, dear radio listeners, this information was translated for us by our colleagues in the London editorial office, so some stylistic inaccuracies are possible. So—Dave's mom. Before the very eyes of the future show-business star. This, of course, became a powerful stimulus ... that is to say left a powerful impression on the young boy, who had not until then experienced anything similar, and led to the creation of his first disk, which immediately went platinum. But we will hear about these and other pleasant things after a short musical pause. (The host pauses.) The music and words of stepan haliabarda. "My mom." Performed by the author.

Stepan haliabarda presses heavily with his hairy little fingers on the keys, I can feel on my skin how he moves his thick, hairy, red appendages, making a mess on his plastic synthesizer and he begins to sing. "I asked the wind, by the gates," he sings, "have you seen, ta-ra-ram, my mom. Go, something ta-ra-ram through this gate, there I saw ta-ra-ram your mom." "Your mom, your mom," the choir sings darkly.

"What's that—a choir?" I ask turning.

"A choir," replies Vasia uncertainly.

"Yeah? And I thought that stepan haliabarda was singing by himself."

"It's a choir."

"What's a choir?"

"stepan haliabarda's a choir," says Vasia.

"How's that?"

"It is. Just listen."

"Your mom, your mom," stepan haliabard sorrowfully voices agreement from the cosmic depths.

"You know," I say, "if it is a choir it's not a nice choir. It's some kind of mean choir. Do you hear what they're saying about mom?"

"Your mother," stepan haliabarda's threatening tone can be heard once more.

"I have the feeling," says Vasia, "they're listening to us."

"Uh-huh, as though they've pricked up their ears, you hear how they've gone quiet?"

"They're spying on us."

"That's hardly possible. What do they need to do that for?"

"Don't know. Maybe they're from the militia."

"Yeah, they sound mean."

"I'm telling you," Vasia says with greater confidence, "it's the cops, a hundred percent it's the cops. Do you hear how they've gone silent, the bastards."

"Wait," I say, "don't get worked up. How can they be cops? Cops don't sing."

"Oh, they don't sing. They sing alright. Have you ever watched the news."

"What?"

"The news."

"Ah. No, I haven't."

"Me, I've watched it," says Vasia. "They showed Mongolian militiamen. On their independence day, singing."

"What—all of them?"

"Well, no, not all of them. A choir. Just like this one here," Says Vasia pointing at the cool radiola. "They were standing, the beasts, and singing."

"And so?"

"And so it's the same thing here. It's the cops, believe me."

"Give me a break."

"I'm telling you."

*20.06.93 (Sunday)*

*0.05*

"I want to sleep."

"You can sleep in the electric train."

"Oh, yeah," I say. "In the electric train. At this time of year the carriage will be full of demobilized soldiers. Or mushroom-pickers. Or militiamen."

"A carriage full of militiamen?" Vasia asks skeptically. "Well, I don't know, I don't know."

"Fine, let's go," I say and we collect our things, preparing to leave.

Cocoa opens the door for us, did you understand? he asks again—to Kintseva, transfer there, exit at Vuzlova and you're nearly there, just a couple of hours—he adds and hands us a brochure of some kind, what's this shit? asks Vasia, take it, says Cocoa, and let the Lord's revelation be with you. What a moron, says Vasia, when the door closes after us, uh-huh, I say, a moron, we go down and on the ground floor by the lift we see Dogg. Dogg, I call, listen, he appears to be dead, wait a moment, Vasia reassures me, walks up to Dogg's body and turns him over face up—Dogg is covered in vomit, but still alive, a little longer and he would probably have died, he would have choked on his own vomit, a real Hendrix, what else can you say, how would he have appeared before the Lord then—with white shoelaces in his army boots and covered in vomit, we pick him up, Dogg, we say, Dogg, wake up, he comes to, even recognizes us, I got lost, he tells us, went out, got some vodka, came back—but I didn't know where to go, I sat here, waited for one of you to come out, where's the vodka? asks Vasia, I drank the vodka, says Dogg, the rain came, it was cold, I thought you would come out looking for me, fine—Vasia says disappointedly—can you walk? yeah, everything's okay—Dogg gets up and we go out onto Gogol Street.

*0.30*

"What shall we do?" asks Vasia.

"Let's go home," I say.

"And Carburetor?"

"What about Carburetor? Carburetor's doing fine. But this one here isn't going to make it anywhere for sure. You're not going to drag him on your back all the way to Vuzlova?"

"Everything's okay," says Dogg. "I'm fine. I can make it."

"Maybe we should go home?" I ask.

"No," says Dogg. "Anywhere but home."

"Fine," I say. "But how are we going to get there. We have no money left, in any case."

"We should have borrowed some from that moron," says Vasia.

"I don't want to borrow from him," I say.

"So, what shall we do?"

"Listen," says Dogg suddenly, "Marusia gave you something for Molotov, didn't she?"

"Right," I say. "I completely forgot." I look in my pocket and get a fairly normal twenty from there. "Cool," I say. "Looks like we have a pile of money. Only we need to exchange it. And not spend it all."

*0.45*

We exchange our twenty in a kiosk not far away, and don't even have time to count up the sum in the equivalent national currency when a militia patrol comes up to us. They don't even ask for documents. It's the natural cycle.

*1.25*

"Sonny?"

"Mykola Ivanovych ..."

"I told you not to repeat this."

"Mykola Ivanovych, I'll explain everything."

"What the hell are you going to explain?"

"Mykola Ivanovych ..."

Fine, says Mykola Ivabocych to the patrol, I'm taking them, is this with you? he asks pointing to Vasia and Dogg, with me, I say, with me, and this vomit-covered one, he says pointing to Dogg again, is he with you? with me, I say, well fine, let's go to my place, I'm taking them, he tells the patrol one more time, I'll talk to them in MY office, is that clear? comrade captain, says the patrol, we brought them in to kind of fulfill the plan, fuck off, Mykola Ivanovych says to them, is that clear? clear, says the patrol sorrowfully and goes out for more hunting, they have a plan to fulfill after all.

"So, here's the story—you two sit here in the corridor, and wait. And you," he points to me, "follow me."

"Okay," I say and enter an office covered with propaganda. "How many posters do you have here?" I say.

"Keep on talking, you prick." Mykola Ivanovych is irritated. "Keep on talking. I'll give you posters, you prick. What did I tell you? If I set eyes on you again I'd kill you. Right?"

"Yes."

"And?"

"Mykola Ivanovych …"

"What?"

"Forgive me. I wasn't going to drink today. You see… We're straight from the funeral."

"From where?"

"From the funeral."

"What funeral?"

"The dean …" I squeeze out of myself.

"What?"

"The dean," I say. "He died on Friday. They buried him today. We helped at the cemetery. You know, to dig the pit, cover the body."

"Seriously?" Mykola Ivanovych asks in confusion.

"Uh-huh."

"And why are you walking around without shoelaces?"

"But you took them from me, Mykola Ivanovych."

Mykola Ivanovych is silent and sorrowful for a long time, but doesn't return the shoelaces.

"Oh, sonny, sonny. What am I to do with you?"

"I don't know," I say. "I don't have any money. The dean's dead."

"What did they call him at least—your dean?"

"Who the hell knows?"

"What?"

"Well, his surname was one of those, you know …"

"I understand," says Mykola Ivanovych thoughtfully.

"What a fucking lousy country we live in!" Mykola Ivanovych says suddenly. "People are dying like flies. My son has been taken to reanimation."

"How do you mean—reanimation?" I ask.

"It turns out that three days ago during the night he broke into a drug store. Says it was for vitamins. Well, I know what kind of vitamins they were, you won't fool me with MY experience."

"And?"

"Well, he crawled in through a small window, grabbed some kind of pills, ate a whole pack, and when he was crawling back he lost consciousness. So he was stuck there."

"Oh, God," I say.

"Yeah," Mykola Ivanovych pensively examines the propaganda behind my back. "In the morning people came to the drug store, found him hanging in the window, not breathing. Well, they took fright, thinking—that's it, the man's dead, then they came closer and noticed that he was still breathing."

"Great," I say.

"What's great? When he was crawling back, he wrenched something in his body, and he was wearing a short coat, imagine—MY coat, in a word, he got stuck—couldn't move forward or back. And he was high on top of it all."

"And so what happened?"

"Well, they called emergency. They said—we can't pull him out of there, he'll get cut up or strangled, so what's to be done? they asked the emergency people what to do and they said we don't know what to do—let him hang there until he falls out himself, but he's high, the first said, if he's high, said emergency, then feed him a bit at a time so he doesn't die there. And those fools, imagine, really did begin feeding him. Well, the under-aged jerk naturally needed nothing more, he wasn't even thinking of crawling out of there, imagine—he could just hang there in someone else's jacket and people would feed him narcotics."

"Class," I say.

"Yeah," says Mykola Ivanovych... "What class? This pup didn't even give them his name. I come home from my rotation and my wife is shouting—our son's disappeared. Imagine? It's a good thing that the next day they found MY documentation in his pocket."

"What were they doing going through his pockets?" I ask.

"They regretted losing the pills, that's what I think. In any case, the next day toward evening they found me. So, together we dragged him out."

"They sent him to reanimation after you?"

"What are you saying?" bristles Mykola Ivanovych, "you think I beat him?"

"No, of course not."

"I never beat him at all. I can't bring myself to beat him. He's simply suffering from dehydration, understand? he was on those pills almost two whole days."

"That's quite something," I say.

"Yeah," adds Mykola Ivanovych pensively.

*2.05*

"Do you know him or something?"

"Yes, we met once."

"Some acquaintances you have."

"You should thank me for getting us out. We'd be sitting in the cell right now."

"He even took the last of the cognac. What will we do now—without cognac?"

"You get heartburn from it anyway."

"Fine, let's go somewhere. Because there's some sort of lets-celebrate-the-commandant hour going on here," and Vasia drags me from the militia station entrance.

Wait, I say, I have to take a leak, later, Vasia says edgily, you can take a leak later, I can't, I say, I walk around the corner of the grey building crammed with gas chambers, and don't have time to even do my dirty business when Mykola Ivanovych comes running around the corner, rushes off somewhere, but nonetheless notices me, sorrowfully nods his head, says, sonny, and runs off somewhere into the night.

*2.35*

We get to the railway station without incident, the taxi driver turns up his nose the whole way and airs out the cab, this agitates the vomit-covered Dogg, but we restrain him, near the suburban station he begins to shout that we shouldn't pay this son-of-a-bitch anything, that he's been giving us the evil eye all through the ride, oh, I tell Dogg, he's put a curse on you, fine, calm down, the driver's frightened, Vasia also tries to pacify Dogg, we pay what we have to and go to the station.

*3.45*

The electric train is very, very slow, the carriages are cold and empty, the floors have obviously been washed, or more precisely—not washed but have had a generous amount of cold dirty water poured over them, we're shaking, we ask Dogg to run and buy something to eat in the kiosk, Dogg buys two litre-and-a-half bottles of mineral water and now he's holding them, we're sitting in an empty cold carriage, there are no mushroom-pickers, no demobilized soldiers, not even any militia, the whole militia is now completing its plan somewhere in the Kyivsky district, where there are still a few living people left, at least someone who can be dragged off to the gas chamber, we survived our commandant's hour, and are now stubbornly attempting to travel to some nowhere land, anywhere.

There are only children moving about the carriage, when we entered they were already sitting there, they arrived from some depot, Vasia and I would never have frightened them, I think they aren't afraid of anything at all, they give the impression of having already lived through everything, including death, but when they see the angry vomit-covered Dogg they shrink into a fearful group, where are you from? Vasia asks, and they begin to tell some story about living here in the electric train, spending the nights in carriages, especially now when it is raining, they travel to Kintseva, then return to the city, sometimes they spend the night at the militia station, but the militia usually lets them go to prevent them from bringing various infections into the cells, and that's how they live, not badly, in fact, not the worst case.

They finally get up and go to the neighboring carriage. For them it's like walking from the kitchen to the living room, they have occupied the train and travel one and the same route as though bound by a spell, or curse.

I try to sleep, but am constantly thrown out of my dream like a poor surfer off a wave, and I begin to groan quietly.

"What is it? Are you feeling ill?" asks Vasia.

"My kidneys are hurting for some reason."

"Yes, the train has shaken you about."

"Uh-huh, it has. Of course, it has."

In those short minutes when I am able to get up on my wave, stand on my board and fly down, I dream of two angels—one is fuller, the other is taller, they walk out into the corridor and begin beating one another, the feathers fly, and their long womanly nails, with which they scratch one another's faces and under which the salt of heaven is congealed, flash in the air like blades in the hands of expert tailors, they strike each other on the face, and their fists are already smeared in blood, and suddenly one of them falls, beats his head against the cold tiles of the corridor, and the taller one—the victor—approaches him and kisses him on his rather full bloody lips, from which a pasteurized milk begins to flow.

I dream that I am the lungs of this angel, I feel how long and diligently someone has beaten him—my angel—precisely on the part of his full body in which I find myself, with heavy football boots, I turn over slowly in his body, I am covered in bruises and wounds, milk comes out of my wounds, I try to turn away from the blows, but I simply have nowhere to turn, because I am completely dependent on the one in whose body I find myself, who covers me with himself, and who uses me continually, all I can do is suffer and observe how this milk comes out of all my pores, out of every cut, out of every torn wound, out of every scar, comes out of me together with my pain, together with my fear, together with my life.

I dream of my angel, who is already dead, he is being transported somewhere, so that his dead defeated body can be burned, he is being dragged along the black floor of the morgue like a dead chicken, the blood and the milk have mixed with his feathers and leave a bloody trail, he is pulled into some big room, placed on a metal table and the rest of his clothing is removed—they take off the black accountant's elbow sleeves, they take off the grey business suit, they take off the Italian shoes, they take off the black socks, the blue shorts, the white T-shirt, someone finally gets a scalpel and makes an incision in the body, cutting it open from the throat to the belly and examines his damaged and exhausted internal organs, devoured from inside by ants, bees, and spiders, and filled instead with fatty pasteurized milk. The incision follows a drawing on his skin, the drawing is an old faded crucifixion, a yellow Jesus on a painted green cross. The scalpel has hardly touched Jesus—but the crucifixion has been cut in half, so now the dead chest cage probably has to be sown together if one wants to have an idea of what it all really looked like.

*4.40*

We do not get out at Chuhuiv. Somewhere in the city at this time, I think to myself, Cocoa's stout and sweaty body has turned over. If he could see us, he would curse. But in Chuhuiv the electric train stops for a minute and a half, the station in Chuhuiv on this disturbing night is wet and unwelcoming, and I wouldn't leave my carriage even if it were to stand here a whole day and a half, although this in no way excuses me in the eyes of the Donbas intelligentsia. In any case, we don't get out. Nor does anyone else.

*5.30*

At Kintseva we want to find at least a bench on which we can wait a couple of hours for the next electric train, but the demobilized soldiers really do start to show up along with the mushroom pickers, all the benches in the waiting room are occupied by some suspicious subjects, so we walk out onto the only platform, over the radio for some reason they speak of it with feeling as the first, as though a second existed somewhere, about a hundred meters from the station a tall passenger bridge can be seen, it overlooks this entire panorama, cool, I say, let's go on the bridge, in any case we have nowhere to sleep, we go up the metal stairs and survey the territory, the endless forks in the railway lines, the freight trains shunted together, cisterns, gravel, semaphores, trees, fog, station buildings, there is so much of everything but nothing to talk about, so we sit there in silence in the fog and clouds and survey all this crippled railway infrastructure, slowly drinking the cold mineral water.

*7.25*

Finally, our electric train arrives, we push our way through the sleepy demobilized crowd and set off in the direction of Vuzlova. Life continues for another two hours. Two normal morning hours, why not?

It's a pity one can't sleep, I, for example, can't sleep in a vertical position for long, it humiliates me or something, it's really rough either way, whether you sit and sleep or stand and sleep—well, you know what I mean—and on top of it all the weather begins to turn bad, clouds crawl in from everywhere, everything seemed so good—the fog, the rails, the cisterns, and now this total loss, we're going to have rain again, this long drudgery from the heavens falling on our heads, I look out the window in agitatation, but everything is completely obvious—it's about to begin, in a moment, in a moment, it's simply ugly to look at the whole thing, I don't know how to explain it—I always take a change of weather personally, as an indignity aimed at myself, although from the weather's side, I suspect, there's absolutely nothing personal about it, well, but I have my own opinion on the matter. The only thing left to do is read. Vasia takes two brochures out of his pocket, he, it turns out, has been dragging two brochures around with him, now he's examining what is written there, passes them on to me, then to Dogg, but nothing good comes of this because there are three of us, after all, and only two books. I even have time to read one.

*Book No. 1*

## EXPLOSIVE JELLY

*(The Laborer's Library)*

*ANNOTATION*

*Dear Friend!*

*You are holding in your hand an extremely interesting and instructive book containing materials that, if correctly assimilated, will help you understand not only theoretically but also practically the principles and tendencies of development of the social-productive relations in contemporary society. Developed and written by the humanitarian-technical section of the party's Donetsk oblast committee, this book will become your best friend and adviser as you take your first steps toward adhering to the inexorable dialectical process and the permanent collapse of capital, insightfully forseen by comrade Trotsky, L.D.*

*It is recommended for home reading and also for collective study in professional-technical groups, labor collectives, places of imprisonment, labor and leisure camps.*

*For children in the middle and higher school years.*

*With regards—the Party of Ukrainian Communists*

## INTRODUCTION

*In place of an introduction. Part 1*

## EXPLOSIVE MATERIALS, NECESSARY FOR THE LABORER AT THE FIRST LEVEL

*1.1*

Comrade!

Make napalm!

Napalm is an inflammatory mixture. It is made of petrol, oil, and aluminum powder. The ingredients necessary for making napalm can and must be obtained at the factory, in the household, or stolen.

*Advice for preparation*

Comrade! The explosive mixture is utilized for the destruction of an opponent's personnel and technological capacity. It is best employed against personnel. In addition, napalm easily burns through even the armature of a tank, if the opponent has one. Moreover, the preparation of napalm can be done by EVERY schoolchild—since napalm, as you already know, is simply a mixture of petrol (2/3), varnish or oil (1/3) and aluminum powder (the more aluminum powder, the stronger the power to burn through objects, remember this!). It is most often used as fuel for flame-throwers or in incendiary bombs.

Note: If you have a flame-thrower, we recommend using this very mixture. A flame-thrower can and must be obtained from military parts, the household, or captured from guards.

*1.2*

Comrade!

Prepare a magnesium explosive!

Magnesium explosive is an explosive of middle power. It consists of magnesium powder or magnesium filings. You have manganese, and magnesium powder or filings can and must be found in factories, warehouses, or in shops serving the people's economy. They can be stolen.

*Advice for preparation*

Comrade! In order to prepare magnesium explosive you need to mix ¾ magnesium powder (filings) with ¼ manganese (proportional to volume). Do not skimp on the manganese, comrade! The mixture explodes with an open flame lasting several seconds (from 2 to 10). During the explosion a bright manganese flash appears, much brighter than a photoflash, and a large amount of white smoke is created.

*Note.* Under no circumstances look at the flash, in the worst circumstances this can lead to total blindness. In principle, it is better also not to look at photoflashes, although this creates some problems for photography.

Even in small quantities magnesium explosive is very dangerous, for example, aerosol canisters filled with it can tear a human being into small colored pieces if the individual is closer than two meters from the explosive.

If further away—they will simply be killed.

*1.3*

Comrade!

Make a Molotov cocktail!

A Molotov cocktail is not a real cocktail; it is an explosive mixture. The cocktail consists of petrol and oil.

*Advice for preparation*

This incendiary bomb in successful circumstances causes an object set on fire. A "Molotov cocktail" is usually a glass bottle (0.5 L or 0.7 L—depending on taste), emptied of its previous drink and filled with two thirds petrol and one third oil. You have the bottle; petrol and oil can and must be removed from economic technology, public transport, or captured from guards. The fuse for the cocktail is prepared from old cloth rags saturated in petrol and then placed in the neck of the bottle. The rags are cut from old work clothing, banners or other visual propaganda. The bottle is stuffed with a cork and in this form, with a lighted fuse, is thrown in the direction of the object to be set alight. The bomb sets on fire the object, smashing against its surface. The enemy cannot to put this flame out with water.

*Note*: Care must be taken in the preparation and lighting, make sure that the cork tightly closes the bottle and does not allow the creation of any gas fumes that can cause a premature explosion! The bomb is not suitable for setting alight objects that are not hard, since it cannot smash against them, remember this in choosing an object.

*1.4.*

Comrade!

Utilize explosive jelly!

Explosive jelly is an explosive matter. Explosive jelly is made up of vaseline. And petrol.

*Advice for preparation*

Explosive jelly is a mixture of 2 parts vaseline and 1 part petrol; it explodes from the action of an electrical current. You have Vaseline; concerning petrol see 1.3; therefore all that is required is an electric current!

*Note*: Caution with the jelly!

*1.5.*

Comrade!

Here is your gas bomb!

A gas bomb is a bomb made of gas. It is composed of burning gas and air.

*Advice for preparation*

A gas bomb is used for destroying enemy personnel (deafening, contusion, disorientation). The simplest gas bomb consists of a bottle with gas and air, which is mixed in certain proportions (see below). It is used in demonstrations, pickets, hunger strikes, during meetings, May Day parades, elections and other labor holidays.

Proportions: natural gas 4.7:15, acetylene 2.5:81, propane 2.2:10, butane 1.8:9.

*1.6*

Comrade!

Prepare a plastic explosive!

Plastic explosive is a powerful explosive matter. It consists of potassium chlorate and, most importantly, vaseline.

*Advice for preparation*

For preparation of plastic explosive it is necessary to mix well crushed potassium chlorate with vaseline. Potassium chlorate can and must be obtained in chemical enterprises, in chemical laboratories and directly from chemists. It is difficult to steal. Vaseline, we think, you are familiar with. For utilization, the prepared matter must be well dried. A detonator is required. Work on this!

*Note*: In its dried state this explosive material becomes sensitive to knocks. Even falling from hands onto the floor can cause a detonation. Do not let it fall from your hands, comrade!

*1.7*

Comrade!

If you are unable to do all this, do not worry; just make yourself some powder.

Powder is a weak explosive material. It is composed of potassium nitrate (85%), coal (12%), and sulphur (3%).

*Advice for preparation*

Mix everything.

*Note*: No notes.

*Chapter 2*

## EXPLOSIVE MATERIALS NECESSARY FOR LABORERS AT THE SECOND LEVEL

*2.1*

Comrades!

Make yourself French ammonal!

French ammonal is a weak explosive material. It is composed of stearic acid, ammonium nitrate and aluminum powder.

*Advice for preparation*

French ammonal is a mixture of ammonium nitrate (86%), stearic acid (6%), and aluminum powder (8%). Its explosive properties are worse than the fatherland's ammonal. It explodes in a pressed state. But if you have the possibility of using a detonator, this changes everything.

*Note*: Needs a detonator!

2.2

Comrade!

Tetryl!

Tetryl is a powerful explosive that is usually composed of tetryl (75%) and TNT (25%).

*Advice for preparation*

This explosive has a powerful bursting charge and is extremely dangerous. It is used in the demolition of buildings, in artillery shells, for blasting railway lines and in other building operations.

*Note*: A detonator!

2.3

Comrade!

Do not despair! There still is amatol!

Amatol is a powerful explosive. Amatol is composed of ammonium nitrate (80%) and TNT (20%).

*Advice for preparation*

This explosive is highly powerful and is extremely dangerous. It is used in demolishing buildings, in artillery shells and bombs and just in general.

*Note*: Creates dangerous compounds together with copper and brass!!!

2.4

Comrade!

Make astrolite!

Astrolite is highly explosive (!). It is composed of ammonium nitrate (66%) and hydrazine (33%).

*Advice for preparation*

Congratulation: this is the most powerful of all known explosives! Astrolite has an extremely powerful explosive force (20 times more than tetryl). The speed of detonation is 9 km/s. Because of its power it is not used, for example, by the military, since it degrades four days after preparation. EVERY school student who knows its ingredients can prepare it. The ingredients are ammonium nitrate (used in industry), hydrazine (used in rocket building, pharmaceutics and industry). To make astrolite mix ammonium nitrate and hydrazine in proportions of 2 to 1.

*Note*: The ingredients are highly toxic, holding them in one's hands is dangerous to life. But allowing them to fall from one's hands is even more dangerous.

*2.5*

Comrade!

Make mercury explosive!

Mercury explosive is a powerful explosive matter. It is made of nitric acid, mercury, and ethanol.

*Advice for preparation*

Making this explosive is dangerous to life, not only your own, so it is better not to make it at all. Nonetheless, for making it you need to mix nitric acid, mercury, and ethanol. The mixture is poured into a bottle and now, if you suddenly break this bottle, there will be a fantastic explosion. Try it some time—do it!

*Note*: Very dangerous! Even if you do not break the bottle, you will be poisoned by the mercury fumes (fatally).

*2.6*

Comrade!

Here is one more trick—nitroglycerine!

This trick is composed of sulphuric acid and nitrate of glycerol.

*Advice for preparation*

Sulphuric acid should have a concentration of not less than 95%. The sulphuric acid is poured into an enamel bowl, the bowl is placed onto snow or ice. In the bowl the nitrate of glycerine is gradually dissolved, in the process the temperature should not be allowed to rise above 10 degrees Celsius. After the nitrate of glycerine is dissolved the compound will lose its transparency and will have a similar appearance to milk. Comrades, this is not milk! Now the compound is poured into cold water with ice, after this, one must wait until all the glycerol crystals have dissolved. Then the compound is filtered and thoroughly washed.

*Note*: Very dangerous! Moreover, this explosive is extremely sensitive to heat. Do not warm it!

2.7

Comrade!

Make yourself thermite!

Thermite, comrade, is an incendiary compound. Thermite is made of iron oxide, aluminum powder, and sulphur!

*Advice for preparation*

A metal compound that when burning gives off large quantities of heat—around 3,000 degrees Celsius! This property can be utilized for preparing a powerful incendiary bomb, understand where we are going? To prepare the thermite you need to simply mix 75% iron oxide (rust) and 25% aliminum. The thermite itself burns at a fairly high temperature, therefore sulphur is added, which upon igniting gives a temperature high enough for the lighting of the thermite.

*Note*: Here's why we need the sulphur!

*2.8*

Comrade!

What about superthermite?!!

Superthermite, comrade, is also an incendiary compound. It is composed of petrol, oil, aluminum powder, and iron oxide (rust).

*Advice for preparation*

This incendiary compound burns giving off a very high temperature capable of melting almost any other metal (the temperature at which it burns is almost the same as that of thermite). A very dangerous thing, you should know. All the same, and this is especially pleasant, it can be prepared by EVERY school student. The ingredients are petrol 44%, oil 20%, iron oxide 16%, aluminum powder 20%.

*Note*: Not every student will realize the possibilities, remember this, comrade!

## *Chapter 3*
## A NOTE TO LABORERS: HOW TO MAKE A BOMB AT HOME, WITHOUT ATTRACTING THE ATTENTION OF THE ANTI-POPULAR REGIME

Comrade!

To make a bomb first gather the ingredients. Ingredients necessary for making a bomb can be bought in a shop selling good for the people's economy or captured from the anti-popular regime, without attracting the latter's attention. You will need:

1. Paper (you can get this at places accepting waste paper, pulp processing factories, or you can prepare it

yourself (see the next brochure in the Laborer's Library series)).

2. Nails (long ones, metal things)

3. A thick wire (thick, comrade!)

4. Glue (Comrade! Put your glue to good use!)

5. Strong thread (!)

6. Saltpeter (industry, shops selling good for the people's economy, the anti-popular regime)

7. Fuse (???)

8. Magnesium (anti-popular regime, only the anti-popular regime!)

9. Cartridge 12 calibre (we expect you have this)

10. Rubber band (simply a rubber band)

*Advice for preparation*

Friend! Take 10 pieces of paper (format A4) and cut each of them in half down the long side. Place one strip on a smooth, level, and strong surface (table, chair, floor). Apply a thin covering of glue (starch or silicone) onto the whole surface of the strip. Place the second strip on top and go over it with an iron (not a hot one!) so as to flatten any air bubbles and to press out the excess glue. Repeat the operation until you have used all the strips. Cover the last strip on top especially carefully with glue. Cut a paper section from the cartridge with a blade. Place the removed part at the top of the glued strips (the edges that jut out have to be the same) and twist them onto it. Leave a space of 0.5-1 cm at the end and press together with a thick wire (twist the ends of the wire and cut them off with wire-cutters) in four places on various sides. Above the wires wind 10-15 coils of strong rope.

Hammer in 7-8 small nails (take care not to tear the rope during hammering). Add 5 parts by weight of magnesium powder to 6 parts by weight of potassium nitrite and mix them evenly. Fill with this mixture the whole cut off part of the cartridge, continually packing it down. Once more leave 0.5-1 cm at the end and press together with a thick wire having previously inserted a nail with the head up. Once more wrap a strong rope 10-15 times around it and hammer in up to ten nails. After some time (24-36 hours) carefully wrap the stretched rubber band around the sides of the bombs. In a couple of days take the band off and pull out the nails. In the place where the nails were, insert a fuse. Place it as low as possible, place it in! And leave the apparatus in this condition to dry for close to a week on the central heating or for two weeks at room temperature. After this the apparatus is ready for use.

*Note*: Use it, dear friend, as appropriate, to hell with it!

We, friend, also strongly recommended nitroglycerine. If you are successful in preparing it, our efforts will not have been in vain.

Therefore, before describing this amazing technology, we want to warn you about the necessary security precautions, although we understand that you do not care. All the same we recommend that you do not ignore at least the minimum security precautions. Because nitroglycerine, comrade, is highly sensitive—you cannot even imagine how sensitive. To be honest, neither can we. We advise you to follow the numerous instructions that are provided here, so that if you are blown up, at least the pieces of your proletarian rags can be collected together. So—to business, comrade.

1. Pour 13 ml of nitric acid that is vapourising into a 75-ml test-tube (98%).

2. Place the test tube into a bucket of ice and give it time to cool to a temperature lower than that of the room.

3. When the nitric acid cools, add three parts sulphuric acid (99%)—39 ml. Mix the acid very carefully, do not allow it to spill.

4. After this you need to lower the temperature of the mixture to 10-15 degrees Celsius, adding ice.

5. Add the glycerine. You must do this very carefully with the aid of a medicine dropper until all the surface of the liquid is covered in a layer of glycerine.

6. Nitrating is a very dangerous stage. During the reaction heat is generated, therefore keep the temperature at the level of 30 degrees Celsius. If it begins to rise, immediately cool the mixture!

7. In the first 10 minutes of the nitrating careful mixing is necessary; try to avoid touching the sides. In a normal reaction the nitroglycerine will create a layer on the surface.

8. After successfully nitrating the liquid it must be very carefully poured into another container with water. The nitroglycerene should sink to the bottom.

9. Pour off as much as you can of the acid, without mixing it with the nitroglycerine, and with the help of the dropper transfer it to a solution of sodium bicarbonate (drinking soda). The rest of the acid will be neutralized.

10. With the aid of the dropper remove the nitroglycerine. In order to test the prepared product, place a very small drop on a metal surface and light it. If you survive, you will see that the nitroglycerine flashes with a pure light-blue flame.

11. We recommend that the obtained portion be transformed into dynamite, since nitroglycerine, the stinker, has a bad habit of exploding without any reason.

And remember, they would very much want you not to do any of this! Maybe you do not want to do any of it yourself. But remember that in reality all bombs are divided into two categories—those that you throw, and those that are thrown at you. So take a convenient position for yourself in the decisive stage of the proletariat's battle for its own, son-of-a-bitch, liberation!

*9.00*

Yeah, I think, quite the book. I put the brochure aside, take another, and immediately fall upon the phrase "Words of Jesus Christ," oh, I think, what's this, some stenographic report, then look closely—in fact it says "Glory to Jesus Christ," that's interesting too, I think, although it would be more interesting if it really was a stenographic report, imagine some meeting at some plant at which the chair suddenly announces: and now Jesus Christ has the floor. You have ten minutes. I think that would be quite enough.

"Where do you get books like these?"

"Oof, the one about the bombs I got from Chapai. He had a whole parcel of them. And the one about Jesus Christ Cocoa gave me."

"And Cocoa, where does he get these books?" I ask.

"He," says Vasia, "hangs out with Mormons. Or no, not with Mormons, with those, what do you call them—Baptists."

"What's the difference?"

"Mormons can have several wives."

"That's not for Cocoa," I say. "He's a total moron."

"Yeah," agrees Vasia, "total."

"You know," he tells me after a silence, "I read various religious books, Cocoa brought them too. They're cool, religious writers, in principle. Only it irritates me that whenever they quote the Bible they always write on every page "From Luke," "From John," "From Matthew," understand? It's as though someone was walking through the electric train selling poison and shouting: from cockroaches! from rats! from all wood lice! Understand?"

I look at him in amazement. "From cockroaches" … What goes on in a person's brain?

*9.30*

The rain could be seen as soon as it appeared, up above, even then it was clear that all of it would in a moment appear here, among us, all we could do was wait and, sure enough, the rain began. We run onto the platform and in the direction of the station, near the doors, under the roof stands a crowd of insane morning passengers trying to get away somewhere from their Vuzlova, the rain becomes more and more dense, falls on us, falls on the station, on the electric train in which we came, on several men in orange jackets who walk along the platform and seem not to notice all this rain, all this crowd, I suddenly think that in reality the rain isn't so cold, it's a good rain, a good summer rain that's falling, where else should it fall, why get all worked up about it, and I go under the nearest trees that are growing alongside the railway building. Vasia and Dogg trail after me, we stand under some pine tree and look from under the branches at the clouds expanding and contracting over the endless railway tracks, coming from the north and south, east and west, leaving behind wet cisterns and cold streams in the drain pipes, and when all this ends, about half an hour later.

*10.00*

When the rain stops and a nice summer morning begins, a holiday, by the way, some invalid, or maybe just an alcoholic, I don't know which—obviously simply a drunken invalid —walks out of the railway station, in one hand he's carrying a small chair, and in the other some box, he puts the chair down on the platform, sits down and puts the box down in front of him, opens it up and—amazingly—it turns out to be a record player, a real old record player, the kind you see on television, in short, the invalid takes out some record, begins to turn something and the machine suddenly begins to work, who would have thought it, he looks around contentedly at all the demobilized soldiers and all the men in orange jackets, but no one is shocked, or asks who this invalid is and what is this record player he has on this platform, then the invalid notices us and understands—if someone can see him in this bestiary then it must be these three sleepy, wet, unfortunate fools—which is to say us—and he smiles at us as if to say—come on, lads, come over here, let's listen to heavenly melodies for invalids and holy fools if you're still capable of hearing such things, come on, come on, don't be afraid. We walk up to him, he continues to smile, well, it's pleasant, whatever you say, we sit down beside him and listen to his rough, scratched and worn out retro vinyl, Dogg also smiles and gets generally emotional, and I think to myself—here are the demobilized soldiers and the men in orange and the wet trees and the cold streams—there doesn't seem to be anything in all this, just normal men, normal demobilized soldiers, normal streams, but all the same I'm sitting here at this moment, next to an invalid whom I don't know, listening to what is basically crappy retro, but there's something right in this, this is how it all has to be, and if you take away the streams or the men in orange —everything would immediately disappear, the joy and the peace are dependent precisely on the great logical unity of thousands of unnecessary, anomalous schizophrenic things, which when combined into a unity give you in the final reckoning a full representation of what happiness is, what life is, and most of all—what death is.

## EPILOGUE No. 1

*10.45*

A patrol emerges from the station, surveys the territory lazily and rests its heavy gaze on the invalid. They come up to the man, exchange some words, the invalid smiles at them in the same vacuous way he smiled at us 45 minutes ago, they press him from both sides, finally one of them, obviously the senior, loses his temper and gives a boot to the record player, which flies to the side and goes quiet.

"We should have taken the invalid," I say to Vasia.

"Taken him where? To the camp? They're locals here, they have to reach an understanding."

"What locals?" I say. "Look at what the bastards have done to the machine."

We are now sitting in the carriage of our electric train, which is just about to set off, and are watching the invalid trying to get up and collect the guts of his record player. But one of the cops, obviously the youngest, quickly runs up to the broken machine and kicks it again with his boot, which makes the record player lift into the air again and, after a heavy flight, land by the station entrance.

"Just a minute," says Dogg.

"Wait," I hold him back. "Where are you going?"

"Hold it, Dogg," shouts Vasia. "We're about to leave."

"Go without me," he shouts and gets out.

"What's with him?"

"I don't know," says Vasia. "Maybe he's feeling sick."

"Let's have a drink and wait," I propose.

"Wait where? What about Carburetor? To hell with him—let him stay here. We'll pick him up on the way back."

*10.47*

The electric train jolts and we set off going further east, but we still have time to see our friend-Jew-Dogg-Pavlov come up to one of the cops, to the senior one, turn him around and punch him right in his sergeant's mug so hard that his cap falls to the ground, and the sergeant himself fall down, and then—we still have time to see—the other patroller rushes to help him, the younger one, and two more run out of the station, maybe even three scum in uniform—we have time to count them—and that is basically everything we have time to see. The electric train leaves, come on, I shout to Vasia the Communist, pull the emergency lever, what are you—an idiot? asks Vasia, what emergency lever, it's only an electric train, that's it, he says, we've passed it.

*10.51*

At first they beat Dogg right on the platform, gradually a crowd gathers around them, the invalid succeeds in running away somewhere, taking the pieces of his retro machine, then the guards drag the unconscious Dogg to their stronghold, handcuff him to a bench, pour water from a bucket on him and begin to beat him again, although there is not much benefit from this—for Dogg for sure. At one point, while he's lying unconscious again on the wet floor out of his throat emerge two tired trout and, beating their tails on the cement floor, they jump under the bench and their silvery broken scales flash.

Toward evening he finally comes to, the sergeant whom he offended has relaxed a bit, fine, he says, you son-of-a-bitch, get going to your Kharkiv, I don't want to see you again, if I do—I'll kill you, together with their pal they load Dogg into the Kharkiv-bound evening express train, warning the conductor not to forget to drop off the body in Kharkiv, the conductor is frightened but what can he do, he doesn't let the bloodied Dogg into the carriage, brings out some water, here, he says, wash yourself, Dogg moves his broken head with difficulty not quite understanding where he is and who he is. And he sits there like that in the entrance to the carriage on the floor all the way to Kharkiv, there the conductor opens the door and helps him get down, Dogg takes a few steps but staggers and barely keeps his balance, then gathers himself and walks off into the city. After an hour he makes it to his granny the veteran, oh, says granny, Vitalik, where have you been? it's okay, says Dogg, everything's okay, and he falls by the fridge.

After two days granny calls emergency. Oh, the doctors say in their turn, he has a concussion, and his collar bone appears to be broken, they carry Dogg's body out into the street and drive him to get some treatment.

In a few days Dogg regains consciousness, the doctors soon get used to him, he stops feeling nauseous, so everything seems to be okay, Dogg even begins to get up from the bed and to go for walks in the corridor, becomes friendly with the staff and generally improves. On Saturday, when there is only one nurse left on duty, Dogg crawls into the office of the section head, finds some spirits there, vitamin C and some other pills, and downs all this on the spot—in the office of the section head.

The following morning they find Dogg on the office floor with saliva trickling from his mouth, they start to pump him, and after pumping him clean they think: what are we going to do with this bastard. The offended staff refuse to let him stay with them.

Dogg spends the summer in a madhouse. He quickly puts on weight and goes wild, a real wild Dogg, a dingo, he lets his thick black hair grow, during the day he walks in the hospital garden and collects apples. Dogg brings these to his neighbors, he doesn't eat them himself, for some unknown reason. One day Dogg meets Chapai in the madhouse. The latter is walking and concentrating on something, he's wearing sports pants and torn sneakers, and is carrying a lunch bag in his hand in which the neck of a bottle can be seen. Chapai doesn't recognize Dogg.

In September the doctor summons Dogg, well, then, he says, Vitaliy Lvovych, we're fagged out with treating you here—something like that, maybe not in those words but something close—we're fagged out, he says, with treating you, so get your stuff together. Where to? Dogg asks in a tired voice. Well, says the doctor, you don't have a large choice—you can either go to prison, but not for long, of course, or to a construction battalion. I don't want to go into a construction battalion, says Dogg, I have these, what do you call them—religious convictions. What convictions? the doctor doesn't understand. Religious, says Dogg. I'm a Mormon. A Mormon? asks the doctor again. A Mormon—says Dogg with less conviction. That means prison, says the doctor. Dogg chooses the armed forces. The doctor lets him back into the ward, thinking, all the same there's a bad smell from this patient's mouth.

I never saw him again.

## EPILOGUE No. 2

*11:15*

"Is he a friend of yours?"

"Yes."

"A nice boy. It's a pity about him."

"A pity," I say. "But what could we do?"

"I'm not saying anything. Just that it's a pity."

"Maybe he'll be released?"

"Maybe," says the lady and stops talking. She has been travelling with us all the way from Kintseva, and also waited at the station for two hours, now here she is sitting opposite and talking.

"Take some," she says unexpectedly and pulls an enormous rubber hot-water bottle out of her bag.

"What is this?" I ask.

"Spirits."

"What, pure alcohol?"

"Yes. Pure."

"Where did you get this?"

"I brought it from Poland."

"Poland?"

"Yes. I travelled there," says the lady, "took some goods, sold almost nothing. It was a pity to leave it, so I'm bringing it back. Take it, you can drink to your friend."

"No," I say, "there's no need."

"Take it, take it," says the lady and turns from us to some acquaintances of hers on the neighboring bench.

I take the hot-water bottle and show it to Vasia as if to say—what do you say, shall we take a shot for Dogg's deceased soul? whatever you say, we failed to save our friend the anti-Semite, take a shot, take a shot, agrees Vasia and gets the half-empty bottle of mineral water. I open the hot-water bottle and pour from it into the mineral water, roughly an equal proportion, although the carriage is shaking so there's no way to be exact, I close the hot-water bottle and we start to drink.

*11.45*

"Is there a toilet here?"

"What toilet? There isn't even an emergency lever."

"I have to go."

"Do it on the way."

"Don't you understand? I have to go!"

"I understand everything. Why are you shouting?"

"When is the next stop?"

"How do I know?" I tell Vasia. "I'm here for the first time, and, I hope, the last."

"The next stop will be in about 20 minutes," says our acquaintance the smuggler. "I'm getting off there. But this stop is only for a couple of minutes. So you won't have time," she laughs.

"You hear," I say to Vasia. "You won't have time. So come on, go to the carriage entrance."

"I can't in the carriage entrance," says Vasia.

"Why?"

"I can't. Understand?"

"No."

"I can't do it that way."

"Well, then wait," I say.

"I can't wait either."

"Stop it," I say.

"Don't you understand?" Vasia keeps repeating.

*12.05*

"That's it, I'm getting out."

"Wait," I say. "There's only 15 minutes left to ride. Hang on."

"No," says Vasia.

"Stop it," I say. All we need is to lose him too. "Carburetor's there."

"I'm getting off," says Vasia.

"You're an ass," I say.

"You're an ass yourself," answers Vasia and gets off, following the smuggler on some nameless station.

*12.25*

"When is the next train to Vuzlova?"

"At two. Only it doesn't stop here. It stops at Chemist."

"And is it far to Chemist?"

"Ten-fifteen kilometers."

"So how do I get to Vuzlova?"

"Well, get on the main road, raise your hand—maybe someone will give you a lift."

Vasia thanks some tipsy muzhyk, whom he has been giving a hard time for several minutes here at the station, and goes looking for the main road. The road is broken and empty, it doesn't look as though anything drives through here, Vasia sits down on the side and starts to wait.

In half an hour a milk truck stops next to him. Where do you need to go, countryman, ask the guys in the cabin, I don't give a fuck, I need to get home, well, okay, they say—get in, Vasia crawls in and they roar off, what are you carrying? he asks in his turn, spirits, laugh the muzhyks, seriously? seriously—spirits, we're out here dodging the customs officials, fantastic, says Vasia, fantastic, he leans against the door and immediately falls asleep, that's it, he hears about an hour later through his dream, we made it through, through what? he doesn't understand, the border! laugh the muzhyks, what border! the Russian border, countryman! and where are you heading? Vasia at last wakes up, to Belgorod, they laugh, to Bel-go-rod, you know a town like that, countryman?

## EPILOGUE No. 3

"Okay, quick, everyone turn out your pockets.

"Yeah? And what else should we turn out for you?"

"I said—turn out your pockets! Otherwise you'll all have problems."

"What are you talking about."

"What's up—didn't you understand?" the guard comes up to Little Chuck Berry and knocks him onto the chairs with a hard blow. No one dares defend him. The other guard stands by the entrance and doesn't let anyone in.

"Quick," says the first one. "Turn out your pockets."

"What are you after?" someone asks.

"A watch."

"What watch?"

"A gold one," says the guard. "A gold rolex."

"And what's that to do with us?"

"No one has been in here except you," says the guard. "While this American moron went for lunch, the room was open, and apart from you no one was in here."

"What the hell do we need his rolex for?"

"The pockets," says the guard and suddenly turns to Cocoa. "Turned out your pockets!"

"What?" Cocoa asks in terror.

"I said—turn out your pockets."

Cocoa remains silent. The guard walks up to him, puts his hand in the pocket of his sandy colored jacket and suddenly takes out a heavy gold rolex. You son-of-a-bitch, he says and hits him with a hard blow in the stomach. Cocoa falls to his knees and begins to vomit right under his legs.

## EPILOGUE No. 4

*12.15*

Sitting here in this carriage full of children and speculators, sitting on a hopelessly hard bench, looking in the window and choking on spirits, I already know now, at the age of 19, what I will be thinking about in ten years time, I know what I will be thinking about, but the main thing isn't even this—the main thing is that I know what I will never think about, never in this world, not a single time, even accidentally. I will never think that everything could have been different, that everything depended on me and was in my hands, that it was really I who created my path and governed circumstances around me, this I will never think in my life. Everything has to be just like this, like this and no other way, and even this might never have been, it's a great happiness that everything happened at least somehow, more or less came together, after all, to be honest, I didn't even count on this, I didn't count on anything, I didn't believe that all this could unwind itself and keep going, I always had the feeling that it could all end quickly and simply—simply now and simply here. Because now and here—at the age of 19, on a hopeless bench, I know what I will believe in 10 years time, I know what I will believe in, and I also know what I will not believe in, I think that in my case little will change, there are things that don't change, precisely because they are related to beliefs. I don't believe in memory, I don't believe in the future, I don't believe in providence, I don't believe in heaven, I don't believe in angels, I don't believe in love, I don't even believe in sex—sex makes you lonely and vulnerable, I don't believe in friends, I don't believe in politics, I don't believe in civilization—but it's better to take things less globally: I don't believe in church, I don't believe in social justice, I don't believe in revolution, I don't believe in marriage, I don't believe in homosexuality, I don't believe in the constitution, I don't believe in the holiness of the Pope in Rome, even if someone were to prove to me the holiness of the Pope in Rome I wouldn't believe in it, on principle I wouldn't. However, I do believe—not even believe—I know about the presence up there above, precisely there where the weather occasionally changes from good to bad, I know about the presence of the one who has dragged me through life all this time, who has pulled me out of my cursed 90s and left me again—to continue living my life, who didn't let me perish just because, in his opinion, that would be too simple, I know about the presence here in the black heavens above us of our newest Satan, who is really the only one that exists, the only one whose existence I will never question, if only because I have seen how he picked up my friends and threw them out of this life like rotten fruit from a fridge, or, abandoning them, squeezed their pupils out, bit through their windpipes, stopped their hearts, broke their necks, inserted mad melodies into their heads, and bloody alphabets into their palates, poured sickly blood into their veins, filled their lungs with fatty pasteurized milk, flooded their souls with fog and wild honey, from which their lives became the same as their despair, which is to say endless.

I know that everything comes from him alone, because if I have felt alongside me someone's presence, it was precisely his, although personally I needed someone else's presence much more, personally it would have been much more important for me to sense alongside me, in the air around me not only the presence of this son-of-a-bitch Satan, but that of someone more sympathetic toward me, well, but everything worked out just the way it did, just so and no other way, and precisely because of this I'm not ashamed of any of my acts, although there were no acts as such, there was only a moving forward through tight hard air, an effort to squeeze forward through it, to squeeze forward a bit more, a few more millimeters, without any goal, without any desire, without any doubt, without any faith in success.

*12.30*

"Chemist," some local long-term resident tells me, a partisan in the underground who is sitting on a neighboring bench, and I get off. There is no station as such here, simply two pavilions standing in the forest—on one is written "Chemist," on the other "CAFÉ CHEMIST," they should have written "Nescafe Chemist," I think to myself and go to the other pavilion. In the café, by a tall table stands none other than my friend Carburetor, in person, almost the same as I remember him—in some short gay shorts, in a tea shirt, with a thoughtful Mongol-Tatar face. Only all tanned somehow and bitten by something, basically there is forest everywhere here, all kinds of mosquitoes, tarantulas, in general I don't know what kind of chemist you have to be to send you kid for a rest to this place, it's like hard labour.

Carburetor notices me, freezes for a moment, and then his face melts into a wide Ho-Chi-Minh smile.

"Ah, you came," says Carburetor.

"I came, I came."

"Well, it's good you came," says Carburetor.

"And what's this, Carburetor, why so cheerful?" I say somewhat irritably, but restrain myself somehow, I say to myself: what's with you, why are you so harsh? "How are things, Carburetor?" I ask in a cheerful tone. What a moron I am, I think, how can he have any things—his stepfather, in the first place, only has one leg, and in the second, has already shot himself.

"Well, things are okay," responds Carburetor and drinks some smelly compote from a glass. "How did you find out?"

Just look at that, I think, he already knows the whole story.

"Well," I say, "your Uncle Robert told me."

"Really?" Carburetor bites some dried biscuit. "How does he know, I wonder? He never congratulated me on this occasion before."

"What occasion?" I ask.

"On my birthday, of course."

"On whose birthday?" I try to understand.

"On mine, of course," Carburetor contentedly strangles on his biscuit.

"Ah," I say after some thought. "Well, then it's clear."

"And where are the presents?" Carburetor continues to be thrilled.

"Here," I say giving him the hot-water bottle. "Keep it."

"Oh, a hot-water bottle."

"It's not a hot-water bottle," I say.

"Then what is it?"

"Spirits."

"Oh," is all Carburetor can respond.

"Shall we get smashed?" I ask and walk up to the lady behind the cash register. "Give me some compote," I say. "And some biscuits, any kind."

"Are you alone?" asks Carburetor when we have mixed and drunk it.

"Vasia was with me," I say. "But he got left behind. He passes on his greetings."

"I see," says Carburetor, drinking the spirits in small gulps. "You here for long?"

"I don't know," I say. "I'll probably return on the next train."

"What? It'll be here in an hour. We won't have time to sit and talk. Stay a while, you can leave tomorrow. I'll put you in a tent with pioneer boys."

"Pioneer girls would be better," I say.

"We'll go see the river," Carburetor isn't listening to me. "I'll introduce you to the group leaders."

"Are they okay?" I ask.

"They're fine," says Carburetor, gulping the spirits. "Nice girls."

"Okay," say I. "Okay. Have you heard anything from home?"

"No," says Carburetor. "Nothing. And thank God for that."

"Why such an attitude?"

"I've had enough of them," says Carburetor. "Whenever they turn up, the problems always begin. Especially with that one-legged moron."

"Your stepfather?"

"Yeah. You see," he tells me, "I told them to get lost a year ago, said don't come and visit me, I don't want to know you, I said, and they keep coming all the same. I finished with them a long time ago, they don't exist for me, understand? They weigh me down. So, better don't mention them, especially today, it's my birthday today, is that clear?"

"It's clear," I say. "Where can I take a leak here?"

"There," Carburetor points to the door. "In the taiga."

*13.00*

The last electric train to Vuzlova will be here in 45 minutes. If I tell him now, he'll have time to get ready and he'll make it there for about 3. From Vuzlova, I think, he can get home by bus, Uncle Robert said that there is one there. Basically, he can make it. The main thing is to tell him now. To go back and tell him. There's something wrong. Something is breaking me up. What? What will happen if I don't tell him? I'm not exactly sure that I want to talk to him about this. As far as I can see he's doing well, everything's okay at least, so I'm not sure that I have the right to say something at this moment. On the other hand they asked me, what's it to me—all the same it's his stepfather, and his mom wants to see him, I should really tell him, even if he doesn't go there, all the same—I'll do what I have to do. I don't know if I'll feel better after it, my family is normal, after all, my parents are normal, true, I haven't seen them for almost a year, but all the same—his situation and mine are different, so I don't know, I don't know.

I suddenly think about Marusia, how is she, I think, she's sitting there, probably, on the balcony with her arms around Molotov who for some reason resembles her dad the general. Why can't she sit like that with her dad? What prevents her? I don't know, it's just that when you have an apartment with a view of city hall and a garage with a Zhiguli, even a wasted one, you stop noticing such things, you know what I'm saying, you stop registering them, it becomes much more natural to embrace the copper bust of Molotov, the central committee member, than your own living dad, it's so absurd. Carburetor's a different story. In my opinion he's had to eat so much shit in his life that obviously he really doesn't need this extra load—what with his family, his one-legged stepfather, Uncle Robert. In any case that's how it seems to me, but who knows how it really is, I'm just standing here and recounting all these stories, recounting all these conversations the way I remember them, so who am I to judge all this. In a minute I'll go and tell him everything.

*13.10*

"Let's go outside, it's better there."

"Let's go," he says, we walk onto the platform, go to the end and sit at the edge facing east, from where the train should appear.

"How are things here?" I ask.

"Okay," says Carburetor. "It's great. I'll buy a building here one day."

"Here?"

"Uh-huh."

"What will you do here?"

"I'll build a sawmill," says Carburetor. "I'll cut down the taiga. Look how many trees there are here. There's enough to last a whole lifetime."

"Yeah," I say, "you'll marry some pioneer girl. Have a pile of kids."

"Well, no," says Carburetor. "Anything but kids."

"Why?"

"Don't know," he says, "don't know. I don't want them to see all this, understand?"

"Well, you saw it all, didn't you?"

"That's why. I'd rather build a sawmill."

*13.20*

"You know, the water here's very cold. I only swim after noon, when it warms up."

"It's raining today, there's no way it'll warm up."

"Probably not."

"So what will we do?"

"I don't know. We'll wait. It'll have to warm up some time."

"How can you tell," I say, "how can you tell."

*13.30*

"Is there any left?"

"Yes," I say, "not much."

"Leave it for later, okay?"

"As you say. It's your birthday, not mine."

"I don't like my birthday."

"Why's that?"

"Don't know, you see, I always felt strange, well, in childhood, they would all gather around and demand something from me. But the birthday was really mine, understand?"

"Yeah."

"The train for Vuzlova will be here soon."

*13.47*

"Listen," I say, "do you take your pioneers swimming?"

"Yes," says Carburetor.

"And what if the water's cold?"

"It's all the same to them, they're like frogs—they jump in the icy water and swim around. They think it's great, they don't understand that the water's cold."

"Has anyone drowned yet?"

"Who would allow it? Even if you wanted, you wouldn't be able to. It's a camp, understand?"

*13.52*

He breaks a yellow hard bread, here, he says, take some, I take a piece and put it down next to me on the as phalt, from behind the clouds the sun finally appears, in a couple of hours the water should warm up and then one will be able to swim across this river of theirs and have a look, finally, at what lies over there—on the other side of the riverbed, which is all the while by my side, to swim across at least once and have a good look at everything over there, a nice opportunity, but the main thing, by the way, is that the water should warm up, the last train of the day passes by us, the clouds drag after it discontentedly, reality sinks toward the west, like a slide, now the next shot should appear, Carburetor chews his yellow bread in silence, drops fall from the pines onto the plastic coverings over the pavilions, we are the only ones on the platform, I look at the asphalt and see a snail crawling up to my bread, he's tired, exhausted by depressions, he stretches out his distrusting mug in the direction of my bread, then disappointedly pulls it back into his shell and begins to crawl back away from us to the west—to the other side of the platform. I think there's enough road there to last him his whole life.

*January-May, 2004, Kharkiv*

Dear Reader,

Thank you for purchasing this book.

We at Glagoslav Publications are glad to welcome you, and hope that you find our books to be a source of knowledge and inspiration.

We want to show the beauty and depth of the Slavic region to everyone looking to expand their horizon and learn something new about different cultures, different people, and we believe that with this book we have managed to do just that.

Now that you've got to know us, we want to get to know you. We value communication with our readers and want to hear from you! We offer several options:

- Join our Book Club on Goodreads, Library Thing and Shelfari, and receive special offers and information about our giveaways;

- Share your opinion about our books on Amazon, Barnes & Noble, Waterstones and other bookstores;

- Join us on Facebook and Twitter for updates on our publications and news about our authors;

- Visit our site www.glagoslav.com to check out our Catalogue and subscribe to our Newsletter.

Glagoslav Publications is getting ready to release a new collection and planning some interesting surprises - stay with us to find out!

Glagoslav Publications

Office 36, 88-90 Hatton Garden

EC1N 8PN London, UK

Tel: + 44 (0) 20 32 86 99 82

Email: contact@glagoslav.com

**Glagoslav Publications Catalogue**

- *The Time of Women* by Elena Chizhova
- *Sin* by Zakhar Prilepin
- *Hardly Ever Otherwise* by Maria Matios
- *The Lost Button* by Irene Rozdobudko
- *Khatyn* by Ales Adamovich
- *Christened with Crosses* by Eduard Kochergin
- *The Vital Needs of the Dead* by Igor Sakhnovsky
- *METRO 2033* (Dutch Edition) by Dmitry Glukhovsky
- *A Poet and Bin Laden* by Hamid Ismailov
- *Asystole* by Oleg Pavlov
- *Kobzar* by Taras Shevchenko
- *White Shanghai* by Elvira Baryakina
- *The First Oligarch* by Michel Terestchenko
- *The Stone Bridge* by Alexander Terekhov
- *King Stakh's Wild Hunt* by Uladzimir Karatkevich
- *Saraband Sarah's Band* by Larysa Denysenko
- *Herstories, An Anthology of New Ukrainian Women Prose Writers*
- *Watching The Russians* (Dutch Edition) by Maria Konyukova
- *The Hawks of Peace* by Dmitry Rogozin
- *Seven Stories* (Dutch Edition) by Leonid Andreev
- *Moryak* by Le Mandel

More coming soon...

Lightning Source UK Ltd.
Milton Keynes UK
UKHW040029150322
400044UK00005B/1333

9 781909 156845